Over the Verdant Hills

RASPBERRY RIDGE
BOOK NINE

JESSIE GUSSMAN

Acknowledgments

Cover art by Julia Gussman
Editing by Heather Hayden
Narration by Jay Dyess
Author Services by CE Author Assistant

Listen to the unabridged audio for FREE performed by Jay Dyess on the Say with Jay channel on YouTube. Get early access to all of Jay's recordings and listen to Jessie's books before they're available to the general public, plus get daily Bible readings by Jay and bonus scenes by becoming a Say with Jay channel member.

One

Claire stared at the ramshackle old farmhouse. In her memories, it was well taken care of—freshly painted, pristine white, with roses blooming around the bottom, vines climbing up the trellis, and more flowers hanging in glorious displays from baskets on the front porch.

In reality, the paint was chipping, the trellis was broken, weeds grew higher than flowers in the flower beds, and the baskets that hung on chains on the front porch held dried stems from last year.

They reminded her a lot of how her life felt. Funny, she'd never really related to a hanging basket before.

"Mom? Why are we just sitting here? Can we get out?" Dan, her ten-year-old, spoke from the back seat, startling her. She'd been sitting there staring. Interesting how memory had a tendency to gloss over things.

Sometimes her memories made things seem worse than they were, but most of the time, the bad faded and just the good things remained.

After a year of having her husband walk out, she remembered more of the good things than the bad. In fact, she'd taken to writing the bad things down so she could remember why she didn't want to go back to him. The fact that he was a liar and a cheat being numbers one and two.

"Yes, you can get out. We'll go greet Grandma first, and then we'll carry our things in from the car. The moving van should be here tomorrow with everything else."

She hadn't quite had the nerve to rent a U-Haul. So their beds, their dressers, and anything else she felt she needed had been left for the movers to pack.

It had been harder than she'd thought to move out of the home she'd made with her husband and children. Much harder than she'd expected.

"Are you getting out, Mom?" Lana, her thirteen-year-old, spoke up from the back seat, with traces of fear and uncertainty in her voice. At thirteen, she was at a delicate age—that transition between childhood and adulthood—and Claire figured there really wasn't a worse time for a child to go through a divorce and a move, having their whole world upended the way Lana's had been. She figured Lana was probably going to be scarred for life, but what could Claire do about it? She wasn't the one who had cheated. She wasn't the one who had left, even though she probably should have after she found out.

There had been fights and tears and therapy, and more fights and more tears and a lot more therapy, which her husband had slipped and slid his way through. He'd charmed the therapist, and Claire found out later he was having an affair with her too.

She shook those thoughts off. She could lose herself for hours ruminating about how terrible her ex had been. All she had to do was tell people, and they would agree with her. But it didn't solve the problem she found herself in—alone with two children on the cusp of their teenage years and a husband who was an absolute jerk in all ways except that he did pay his child support and alimony.

She could be grateful for little things.

He'd apologized multiple times too, but that didn't change the fact that he didn't seem to be able to be faithful to one woman. And that was a prerequisite for them getting back together.

She'd given up on that idea.

"Yes, I'm getting out. I was just thinking about how I remember this place from when I was a little girl. There were flowers everywhere, and... it looks like Grandma needs some help."

"I hope I don't have to work in the garden," Lana said, sounding peevish.

Funny how she could go from insecure and sounding like she needed her mother's arm around her to sounding like the most rebellious of rebellious teenagers. She supposed that came with being thirteen.

"All right. It has been noted that Lana doesn't want to work in the garden, even though she will be required to do whatever work is expected of her," Claire said, trying to sound kind yet firm at the same time. It was something she wasn't very good at. She was much more of a pushover than a disciplinarian. The children had figured that out long ago, and Claire had required herself to become almost a boot camp instructor in order to get her children to do what she wanted them to do. She couldn't be easygoing and lackadaisical like she wanted to be, not if she expected her kids to obey.

"We don't have to work today though, do we, Mom?" Dan whined in a tone he had perfected during the last ten years. As the youngest, he might have been a little bit spoiled, especially since his dad had always wanted a son. When Dan came along, there wasn't anything Ted wouldn't do for him.

Except stay faithful to his mother.

"Let's go see Grandma, and then we'll figure out what we're doing for the rest of the day. But no, I don't expect you to work today, other than to get our beds made and that type of thing. I don't know how well she's getting around."

It had been a few years since she'd seen her. They talked on the phone a good bit, and her grandma had even figured out how to FaceTime, so she'd seen her, but she hadn't really seen her move around.

After looking at the house, she wondered if her grandma had aged in the same way it had.

Or maybe her memories were just rose-tinted, the way her memories of the house were.

She'd had so many good times here, so much fun with her friends... She didn't really want to think about that, because that brought up the tragedy she had spent her life trying to forget.

A shot of guilt went through her as she recalled that Grace had tried to call her several times. She had screened her calls, and finding out it was Grace, she'd deleted both the message and the number.

That wasn't exactly the act of a friend. It was the act of a woman who was too much of a coward to face the past.

Still, she had enough on her plate, and she didn't need to think about it anymore. Not now, anyway.

She closed the car door behind her and started up the walk with her kids trailing behind her, talking, asking whether they could see the lake, whether there were any animals on the farm, wanting to know where the property line was, where the beach was—all the things.

Claire hated to break it to them, but they were going to school the next day. They'd have to wait for the weekend to properly explore. Before that, she was going to have to show them around the property, because there were several cliffs that could be dangerous, and she wanted to make sure they knew where the boundaries were and that they needed to ask permission before going near the water.

She didn't want another lake tragedy.

Suddenly, she wondered if this was a good idea. After all, she'd been brought up around the lake, and she knew its personality, how psychotic it could be. One minute placid and sweet, the next minute angry and vengeful. Sometimes there was no happy middle, and sometimes it changed without warning.

She had known the strict rules from the time she was small. She never went to the lake without her parents knowing where she was and never by herself.

"All right, guys, make sure you're kind to your great-grandmother. Remember we talked about being respectful and that she's older and probably won't move as fast as what you're used to." Ted's parents hadn't been a big part of their lives, but they were young, energetic, always doing something. They'd gone on several ski trips and Caribbean vacations together. That was probably why Ted didn't have a problem paying the child support and alimony—his parents paid for him.

Regardless, her mother wasn't nearly as athletically inclined, not to mention she lived in New Mexico and they barely saw her.

Grandma was her grandmother, her children's great-grandmother, and her kids weren't used to being around anyone as old as she was.

Hopefully she hadn't aged as much as the rest of the house.

She knocked on the door and then opened it.

"Hello? Grandma?"

"Oh!" a voice from the kitchen said. "Are you here? Was that today?"

Claire's heart sank. Grandma wasn't even expecting them? But she'd called her last night and texted this morning.

"Yeah, it was today. Did you not get my text this morning?" She knew she had gotten it, because Grandma had replied.

"I did. But... I guess I forgot."

Her grandma came out of the kitchen, leaning on a cane and walking slowly.

Definitely a difference from her childhood, when Grandma had been smiling and, if not energetic, at least happy. There had been a cheerfulness about her that had seemed to settle over the entire farm. Of course, since those days, Grandma had lost her husband and had a son die of cancer—Claire's uncle.

Of course, Grandma had been touched by the tragedy that had happened in Claire's youth as well.

"Children, say hi to your great-grandmother," Claire prompted her kids. She wanted them to love her grandma as much as she did, and she supposed that meant she needed to back off, but she appreciated her grandma allowing them to move in, and she wanted to make sure they were as kind to her as they could be. She didn't think her grandma would ever kick them out, not for anything, but she didn't want to take that chance either.

Her kids dutifully went up and gave lackluster "Hi, Grandma"s as they hugged her.

Claire swooped in afterward and gave her grandma a real, honest-to-goodness, I'm-so-happy-to-see-you hug. She truly was. It was good to be back in Raspberry Ridge, good to be back in the old farmhouse that seemed so familiar and loving, even if it had been touched by time. It still brought her back to her youth, when life was carefree and happy. For the most part.

"I'll have to put something together for supper. Don't know why I thought you were coming tomorrow. You're right, I saw your text today."

"Don't worry about it. We just stopped on the way here, and I'll figure out something to make for supper. If worse comes to worst, I can go get some bread and meat and we'll just have sandwiches."

"I have eggs. I still have chickens, although those are the only animals on the farm anymore."

"All right. We can do something with eggs. The kids like them hardboiled, or we can have egg salad sandwiches if you have bread."

"I can whip up a couple of loaves."

Of course. Her grandma always made her own bread. A sigh of longing started at her very soul and whispered from her lips. "Homemade bread sounds amazing."

Nothing said childhood the way homemade bread did. She didn't even need egg salad. She could just eat it with melted butter and down an entire loaf by herself.

That would be just great. She could gain a hundred pounds on her grandma's homemade bread, and the next time her husband saw her, he'd be happy he divorced her in time.

That wasn't very kind, but it was true as far as her ex was concerned. He had insisted she stay in shape and not "let herself go" like so many other women did, according to him anyway.

In her opinion, people just got older, and they couldn't look like they were eighteen forever. They started to look like adults, then middle-aged adults, and then... Who knew what was going to happen after that.

Regardless, he was completely uninterested in anything she deemed important. Obviously, since he felt the shape she was in was more important than the character he had.

"It's so good to have you here. I get lonely sometimes," Grandma said, smiling at her and then putting her hand on Dan's head, although she couldn't reach Lana, who had moved away from her and looked at her like she might look at a snake trying to come out of a hole.

Claire wanted to say something to Lana, to make her be more respectful to her great-grandmother, but she'd probably already pushed the envelope by making them hug her. Eventually they would love her grandma just like she did. Although, come to think of it, she didn't really appreciate her grandma like she should have until after she moved away and lived without her for a while.

"When we've been here a while, you'll probably wish for the good old days when you didn't have a crowd of people running in and out."

Grandma laughed and patted her hand. "I don't think so. This old house needs a breath of fresh air, like you and your children can provide. I'm grateful you're bringing it. Now, should we start on something to eat, or should we go get beds ready?"

"How about you just tell me where the linens are, and I'll get the beds ready myself with my kids' help," she said, emphasizing the last part as she eyed her two children. They weren't going to get waited on hand and foot here, and they might as well accept that now. They'd had a housekeeper in their old house back in Boston, and her kids had grown up doing less than she wanted them to. She'd just gotten tired of the constant fight, because not only did she have to fight her children, she'd had to fight her husband and the housekeeper as well. Not to mention, her husband's parents didn't think the children should have to lift a finger to do anything more strenuous than turn the TV channel.

"I want to go outside and play," Dan said, and it was so close to back talk that Claire hesitated before she said, "You may, as soon as you have your bed ready for the evening."

"You could also gather the eggs for the day if you want to. I haven't done that yet."

"Gather eggs?" Dan said, wrinkling his nose up, like he wasn't quite sure whether it was something he was interested in or a job he wanted to avoid.

"Real eggs?" Lana said. "That come from real chickens?"

"The very same," Grandma said, smiling benevolently at Lana, despite the fact that she hadn't been the nicest. That was the thing about grandmothers—they loved you no matter what. At least, that was the way it was in Claire's experience. Maybe that wasn't the way everyone had it, but everyone should have someone who loved them without them having to be the right size, or the right age, or the right anything. Just the way they were.

That's the kind of grandmother she wanted to be. Of course, at the rate her kids were going, they weren't going to be talking to her by the time they had children.

She didn't want to think about that either. Too many families she knew had children who weren't talking to their parents, and she didn't really understand why. But it seemed like an epidemic.

"Can we do the eggs first?" Dan asked.

"We're going to get beds ready first. Then we'll do the eggs, because we need those for supper, along with the bread."

"Does making bread take a long time?" Lana said, and she didn't sound like she wanted to wait a long time for supper.

"We'll have supper today, so it doesn't take that long," Claire said, sidestepping the question of exactly how long it might take. She'd benefited from eating the bread her grandmother had made multiple times over the years, but she'd never helped her make it.

She didn't know why not.

Well, maybe because she was so busy being outside running around that she didn't have time to come in and help. Maybe she should just let her kids run around wild. It would probably be good for them.

"I have linens in the closet at the top of the steps, and there are beds in three of the six bedrooms."

"Good, because I have two beds coming. I hope that's okay."

"It certainly is. We talked about it, didn't we?" Grandma furrowed her brows as though she were trying to remember.

Was Grandma losing it?

Claire's heart shivered. That was the last thing she needed. She'd wanted to come back here and be grounded, to rest and recover and figure out the rest of her life, not be scared every day wondering whether her grandma was going to recognize her or not. Her grandma was supposed to be a rock in her life, the anchor that grounded her, not another rock that could sink her.

But she supposed she couldn't change that any more than she could change a myriad of other things she'd like to change. Whatever happened, she'd have to accept it and be okay with it.

"All right, thanks, Grandma," she said as she started toward the stairs.

"I'll get started on that bread. And when you guys are done with the beds, I should be in a good place where we can go out and meet the chickens."

Her kids grunted as they started to ascend the stairs behind her.

Claire dug in the linen closet for the sheets and blankets her grandma had talked about.

They smelled clean but old, like they'd been there forever, and she thought she recognized them as sheets she'd used when she'd stayed over as a girl.

She wanted to put the sheets to her nose and breathe deeply, because the scent felt comforting and familiar, even if it brought her a little sadness to think that so many years had gone by.

But her kids already thought she was a little bit nutty, and she didn't want to hold them up on purpose, especially not after such a long trip. They'd broken it down into two days, but it had still been a lot of driving, and they were all tired. The kids wanted to run around, and she couldn't blame them.

So she allowed them to pick the rooms they wanted, and she decided she'd stay in one of the beds that were already set up, but she would put her bed in the bedroom with the windows facing south. It had always been her favorite room, especially since it had sunshine most of the day. That was especially essential during the long Michigan winters that could be dark and cold and rather dreary. Although she recalled being outside in the snow, skiing and ice skating and generally figuring out something to do in order to play with the white stuff that came from the sky.

Wasn't that what kids did? They made toys out of everything.

Regardless, her kids grumbled, and she had to help Dan a little bit, but they were able to get their beds made well enough that they could sleep in them for the night.

Sometime in the next few days, she would have to teach them how to use the washing machine, because she was going to expect them to do their own laundry, including washing their own sheets. If she had to get a job, which she planned to do eventually, she wasn't going to be able to wait on them hand and foot, and she certainly wasn't going to expect her grandmother to do that either.

The kids were going to have to grow up and take care of themselves.

Two

"We finished the beds, Grandma. Can you show us how to do the eggs now?" Dan said as soon as they walked into the kitchen where her grandmother was elbow-deep in a bowl of flour.

"That was perfect timing," Grandma said, shaping the dough into a ball and then rubbing the floury mixture off her hands before she grabbed a cloth and covered it. "Just let me wash my hands, and we'll go outside."

"How many chickens do you have?" Dan asked.

Claire found herself vaguely relieved. She wasn't sure whether she was going to have to explain to her kids that chickens laid eggs and then people ate them. She was pretty sure they knew that, but it was the kind of thing they had never actually seen before or experienced. All the eggs they'd ever seen had come from the grocery store. She was afraid they had no idea how they got there.

"I have twenty." Grandma chuckled. "But only about twelve of them lay every day. I'm just too softhearted in my old age, and I can't get rid of the ones that aren't laying anymore."

"Do you have a rooster?" Claire asked, remembering that she'd had several run-ins with her grandma's roosters over the years and hadn't always emerged as the winner.

"I do. But he's a nice, calm fellow. Although sometimes roosters see things that are about their size and think about challenging them." Her grandma eyed Dan thoughtfully. "We'll see how he takes to you."

"What does that mean?" Dan asked with the subtlety of a ten-year-old.

"That means the rooster might be a little bit aggressive. We'll see." Claire didn't want to scare her kids, but she also didn't want to protect them from the realities of life either.

"Are you saying the rooster may attack us?" Lana said, and she looked like she was planting her feet on the floor and getting ready to absolutely refuse to move.

"I suppose that's a possibility. I've been attacked by roosters and somehow lived to tell the tale. I bet you will too," Claire said, trying to give Lana an encouraging smile, although she gave her a dose of honesty too. What was she supposed to do, lie to her child?

Maybe she could have broken the truth a little bit more gently, because Lana looked even more determined to stay right where she was.

"I don't think chickens are my thing. I'll just stay in here and wait for you guys to come back."

"If you want to do the dishes tonight, I'm okay with it," Grandma said.

Claire hid a smile. That sly old lady. She had manipulated her when she was younger, and she hadn't even known it. But she remembered Grandma saying similar things like that to her and how quickly it had gotten her to agree to whatever Grandma wanted her to do.

Funny, the things kids didn't notice.

"Fine. I can go out, I guess."

"That's great. Then we'll have you and your brother take turns doing the dishes, and you take turns doing the chickens."

"Wait a second. You mean Dan also has to do the dishes?" Lana said, again planting her feet.

"Not every day. You guys can switch off. Whoever gathers the eggs, which also includes feeding and watering the chickens, won't have dish duty in the evening."

"Why don't you have a dishwasher?" Dan said, eyeing the old-fashioned kitchen with its porcelain sink and Formica countertops. The wooden cabinets looked like they were made out of particleboard and painted white about fifty years ago. It could definitely use an update.

"Because I have great-grandchildren who come and wash my dishes for me," Grandma said, acting like it was the most natural thing in the world for her great-grandkids to come and wash the dishes.

It kept Dan from asking about anything anyway.

"This is my gathering basket," Grandma said as she picked it up from where it sat by the door.

It was a lot fancier than what Claire remembered using when she was a kid. She was pretty sure she'd just pulled her T-shirt out and put the eggs in the pouch it made.

Of course, she remembered breaking more than a few, particularly when she ran away from the rooster.

"That's cute," Lana said, and Claire bit back a gasp of surprise. Was Lana actually saying something positive?

Of course a cute little basket might make her want to gather eggs.

"Thanks. I also have an egg-gathering apron, but it's hanging outside on the porch." Grandma walked out, and they all trooped after her. Grandma showed them the egg-gathering apron, and then she said, "I put it on just in case I have to set my basket down. But then I transfer the eggs to the basket, because it makes me feel cute to carry the basket around."

Claire kept from snorting. Maybe when she was eighty-something years old, she'd be carrying a basket around just because it made her feel cute. She figured anything that made her feel cute when she was eighty was something she was going to keep in her life.

Goodness, anything that made her feel cute now was something she would keep in her life.

Her kids tramped after her grandma, and Claire brought up the rear as they headed toward the chicken coop, which was fifty or sixty feet away from the back door.

She recalled the chickens pecking all around when she was younger, but she also remembered that Grandma didn't let them out until it was fairly warm out on a consistent basis. Once that happened, then Grandma had to go out in the evening once all the chickens had roosted and shut the door. Otherwise, predators might get in and eat the birds during the night—particularly foxes or owls.

Funny, the things Claire remembered, and equally interesting, the things she forgot.

"All right, we're all going to pile into the coop, even though it's not very big in there. I only have twenty birds and ten laying boxes. I couldn't fit any more, or I probably would have a lot more. Chickens are a lot of fun to watch."

Her grandma held her cane over her arm as she opened the door to the coop. Then she took the cane, carefully balancing it on the cement block steps as she walked up and into the coop.

It wasn't a pretty prefabricated shed. It was one that had been built on the property years ago, with its weathered boards and dark gray exterior. Claire seemed to remember that one time it had been painted white with green shutters and green trim. But if that memory was correct, the paint had long since faded.

"Close the door behind you," Grandma said to Claire as Claire stepped in last. "I don't want anyone to get out. It's not quite warm enough yet. I've been going to bed earlier and earlier, and I'm not sure I'm even going to let them out this year. Letting them out means staying up later than is comfortable," she said, lifting her brows at Claire.

"Now that we're here, I'm sure I won't have trouble staying up as late as it takes to close the coop."

"I'll keep that in mind," Grandma said.

Then she turned to the children and started instructing them on what they needed to do in order to gather the eggs.

"When it's your turn, you can't shirk your duties. If there's a chicken sitting on eggs, you have to put your hand underneath them and get the eggs out from under them. Otherwise, they're liable to sit on the eggs, and they'll go bad."

"How do we know if there are any eggs under there?" Dan asked, looking curiously at a chicken who eyed him suspiciously from the nest box where she sat.

"You have to put your hand under there and feel around. Usually they're toward the front, but sometimes they put them by their feet.

You'll be able to feel them," Grandma said with assurance. Then, to show them, she stuck her hand underneath the chicken that was sitting there as it pecked at her wrist and arm.

"Doesn't that hurt?" Lana asked as she watched with horror as the chicken practically attacked Grandma's arm.

"Not really. You get used to it. Every once in a while, they get you in a good spot, but their beaks are trimmed so they can't hurt each other, and they can't hurt you either."

"How do they trim their beaks?" Dan asked.

"You do that when they're chicks. There are a couple different ways, but one is a tool that's hot, and it kind of sears the end of their beak. It's like your fingernails, though. It doesn't have any feeling in them."

"I see," Lana said, still looking a little horrified.

"Look. She was sitting on three eggs. This hen probably isn't laying eggs—she's sitting on somebody else's."

"You mean another chicken laid those three eggs?"

"Chickens usually only lay one egg a day. So there were probably three different chickens in this nest, and then this hen got in to sit on the eggs, because she's what we call broody. That's when a chicken wants to sit on eggs and hatch them herself."

"Can we let her do that?" Lana asked, showing excitement for the first time that day. Claire wanted to put her hands over her mouth and thank God that there was some kind of sign of happiness and that life might be worth living from her daughter.

"We'll do that later this summer when it's warm out. If the chicks hatch when it's too cold, they'll die. Now, the mom keeps them warm by keeping them close to her, but sometimes the chicks run away and don't do what they're supposed to. In that case, it needs to be warm enough that they're okay for a few minutes without the heat of their mom."

It was all Claire could do not to close her eyes and smile, savoring the memories of her childhood. Her grandma had told her almost the exact same thing back when she was little. She could remember it like it was yesterday. Coming here definitely felt like the right thing to do.

Grandma gathered the eggs, using the apron, and then she helped the children get the eggs out of the apron and put them in the basket.

Once the eggs were safely in the basket, she handed it to Claire and then showed the kids how to feed the chickens and fill up their water.

Claire stood watching her kids take turns being grossed out and interested.

It solidified the thought she'd had just a few minutes prior—that coming here was the right thing to do. Not just for her, but for her children too. She thought all of them would benefit.

There was a sadness that burdened her heart, just because her husband wasn't there, but... He'd made his choice. Over and over and over again. As much as it broke her heart, there was nothing she could do to make him make a different choice, although she wished she could.

Regardless, it was thirty minutes later when, with her basket of eggs, they walked back into the kitchen.

No sooner had they set the basket down and washed their hands than there was a knock at the front door.

"My goodness. Whoever could that be? This is just the busiest my house has been in years," Grandma said as she got her cane and hobbled to the front door.

Claire almost offered to answer the door for her, but she felt like maybe she would be overstepping just a bit. After all, this was her first day here. Should she act like the house was hers too?

She and Grandma had talked about her paying some type of rent, and Grandma had said that once she got there, they would figure it out. Claire definitely did not intend to stay here without compensating her grandma in some way, although she probably couldn't pay what renting a six-bedroom farmhouse was worth.

It was seven bedrooms if she counted the fact that Grandma had turned the old parlor into her own bedroom.

"Josiah McMurtry," Grandma declared as she opened the door. "I completely forgot that you were here to fix that leaky toilet."

Claire wanted to sink through the floorboards. Josiah McMurtry? Figures he would be the first person she ran into on her first day here.

She slowly turned and realized his eyes were boring into hers.

"I see your granddaughter showed up like you thought she was gonna," Josiah said in his slow, methodical way. "Only I wasn't expecting her until tomorrow."

"My goodness. I just have my days all mixed up." Grandma waved a hand, and Claire wondered exactly what she was doing. She didn't seem to be the slightest bit addled any time except when it came to the day that Claire was going to show up. Had Claire messed up and told her the wrong date? Or was Grandma doing something different?

Regardless, Claire steeled herself to face this ghost from her past.

Three

Josiah stared at Claire Baney.

Well, it wasn't Claire Baney anymore. Whatever her married name was, he didn't know. But she looked just the same as she had in high school, when he'd had a bit of a crush on her. Of course, he'd been skinny with glasses and a nerdy reputation, and someone like Claire wouldn't have looked at him twice. She didn't really look at him twice now, although he'd changed a good bit since their school days. He was one of those kids who hadn't really started to grow until their senior year in high school. He'd filled out a good bit after that too, but of course, Claire hadn't been around to see it.

"Hello, Claire," he said as she continued to stare at him.

She seemed to shake herself.

"Hello, Josiah," she said, looking like she was forcing herself to be polite. "It's good to see you. Unfortunately, I have bread rising in the kitchen, so I'd better go check on it."

He stood there while she turned around and walked into the kitchen.

Then his gaze turned toward Miss Mattie—most people around here called her Grandma.

Miss Mattie shrugged and then said, "That toilet is back here," and she led the way to the bathroom, where he could hear the toilet running long before they got there.

There were a couple of kids watching him from inconspicuous places, and he assumed those were Claire's children. He'd heard she had two, but he wasn't exactly well plugged into the underground gossip vines of Raspberry Ridge, and he wouldn't be surprised if his information was inaccurate.

His mom had suffered from multiple sclerosis since he was in junior high, and he'd foregone college so he could stay and help her and his dad.

His mom was still doing okay, and his dad still worked as a radiology tech at the Blueberry Beach Hospital. And he still hung around, taking care of his mom and helping out around the house for his dad as well.

He supposed most people would figure he had a lack of ambition and look down on him.

In reality, he loved his small town and spent a lot of time trying to figure out how he could earn a living so he could stay right where he was.

"Once you get that fixed, don't you run off. We're having homemade bread for supper and fresh egg salad with eggs I just gathered. I also have eggs for you in a carton on top of the refrigerator. Don't leave without them, and make sure you get yourself some fresh bread, okay?" Miss Mattie put her hands on her hips and gave him her no-nonsense look. He could no more disagree with her than he could back-talk his mom.

"Yes, ma'am," he said, meeting her gaze before he turned back to the running toilet.

It sounded like it might need a new float, and he didn't have one of those with him. But once he got the lid off, he might be able to figure out something else. He ought to at least be able to figure out a way to get it to quit running until he could get to the hardware store and get the pieces he needed.

She'd told him she had a toilet that needed fixing, but she hadn't given him any details.

He'd done a good bit of work for her around the place in the last year or so. It was almost like she was gearing up to host her granddaughter, but if she'd known about it, she hadn't told him.

She had jobs lined up for him through the summer too. One of those included fixing the trellis beside the rosebush on the gable end of the house.

He remembered back when he was a kid, the deep red roses that had climbed up there every spring.

He could still smell them if he thought about it and remember how he thought about climbing up the trellis to Claire.

Not that he'd had an idea to pursue Claire for very long. She'd been pretty clear that she wasn't interested, and somehow her lack of interest had convinced him that he was wasting his time.

It took about an hour to fix the toilet. It turned out it wasn't the float after all, and he was able to use the tools in his bag to fix it.

He'd figured out that he was pretty clever at fixing things and putting things together when he was in junior and senior high. Of course, at that point in his life, he hadn't considered that he might be able to make a living out of it. But it turned out there were millionaires who had large yachts that ran on Lake Michigan, and with just a little bit of advertising—but mostly word of mouth—he'd been able to pick up jobs at the port down in Blueberry Beach. He only needed one or two jobs a month, and then he could spend the rest of his time in the small town he loved.

Interesting the way life worked out sometimes.

He thought that again as he walked into the kitchen and saw Claire in there. He hadn't thought he'd run into her again. There was a lot of water under the bridge, but they did have some history.

Nothing she would probably want to remember, although he thought back on it with fondness.

"And then, once you have the loaves formed, you can put them into the pans you buttered, and then you have to wait for them to rise. Usually takes about thirty or forty-five minutes," Miss Mattie said as he walked into the kitchen.

"I just wanted to let you know I was all done. The toilet's fixed. I thought I would need a new float, but it turned out I had the pieces I needed in my bag."

He'd set his bag by the door, and he'd been tempted to walk out, but Miss Mattie had specifically asked him to stay, and he found he couldn't deliberately ignore her request.

"My goodness, that took hardly any time at all. Come on in. The bread isn't quite ready, but you can sit at the table and catch up with Claire. I think you remember her, don't you?"

"I do. We went to school together," he said, after pausing for a moment to see if Claire would speak up. She was looking at him from the corner like he was some kind of spider that had crawled out of hiding.

It was kind of the way he remembered her looking at him in school too.

But he couldn't change that. He wasn't quite sure what her issue was, although... Maybe he had an inkling. Still, she'd been through a good bit back in school, and he had no idea what she'd been through since then. He could cut her some slack.

"I don't want to stay too long. My dad—"

"Oh, don't you worry. Your mom expects me to feed you, and you told me yesterday that your dad was going to be home tonight, so it was a good night for you to come over and fix the toilet."

He'd said that. It was true. His dad got home early on Thursdays and had Fridays and the weekends off. He worked fourteen- and sixteen-hour shifts Monday, Tuesday, and Wednesday.

"Claire, have you spoken with Josiah since high school?" Miss Mattie was obviously trying to facilitate a conversation between the two of them.

Josiah felt a little bad for her. After all, Claire was obviously not wanting to talk to him. He noted that the boy who had been there earlier was nowhere in sight, but Miss Mattie had been teaching the girl about the bread while Claire stood against the counter, her arms crossed, watching.

"Josiah, go on. Sit down for a bit." Miss Mattie smiled engagingly. "I have some chocolate cake that I was holding back, but... I'll get you a piece. That ought to make waiting a little easier."

He did have a weakness for chocolate cake, and she knew it. Which was why there was cake there, he was sure. He couldn't decline her offer.

"Claire, darling, why don't you grab the cake that's on top of the refrigerator and cut a nice generous piece for Josiah. You can get one for yourself too if you want to. You look like you could use a little meat on your bones."

Miss Mattie wasn't wrong. Claire looked as skinny as a rail. Unhealthily skinny, if there was such a thing, although the more he looked at the weight tables in the doctor's office, the more he felt like being so skinny that your bones stuck out was what they considered healthy nowadays.

When he was younger, he was all elbows and knees and knobby bones that stuck out in odd places. But he'd filled out some and put on some muscle, so he didn't look like a toothpick with elbows anymore. Still, he'd probably never be heavyset.

"It's been a while, Claire," he said as she set the cake down on the table without saying anything.

Miss Mattie set two plates down and the spatula to scoop the cake out with. Claire murmured a thank you, and then she looked directly at Josiah.

"It has. On purpose, for my part."

Okay. He wasn't sure what to say about that. Was she talking about him, or was she talking about being in Raspberry Ridge in general?

"It's good that you're back." He tried to rack his brain for something else to say. "It's pretty this time of year."

The weather. The good old standby when a person couldn't think of anything else to say. And Claire was not exactly looking welcoming at him in any way.

"I suppose," she said, and he didn't know whether she was answering his first comment or his second. Maybe she was combining both answers into one.

This was going to be a long half hour until the bread was ready. He wasn't sure he was going to be able to endure this level of passive-aggressive almost glaring from Claire the entire time.

"You know what, it's pretty warm in this kitchen with the oven heating up and everything, so why don't you two take your cake and go sit out on the front porch? Lana and I will tidy up in here, and then we'll go make sure that Dan didn't wander off. We'll have to talk to him about lake safety soon."

"Yeah, I wanted to do that, but I haven't gotten around to it. I figured after they get back from school tomorrow, we'll—"

"We're going to school tomorrow?" the girl said—what did Miss Mattie call her? Lana? She didn't sound very happy.

Maybe Josiah should thank her, because it made Claire move a little quicker, and she was hurrying toward the front door with two pieces of cake almost before he was able to catch up to her and open the door before she got there.

"Thanks," she said without looking at him as she used her elbow to push the screen door open.

"No problem," he said as he shut the door behind him and then caught the screen so it didn't slam. Miss Mattie had yelled at him years ago when he was a kid for slamming the screen door, and those lessons stuck.

"Here's your cake," Claire said, still not looking at him.

"Is there something I did that made you mad?" he asked, knowing that he hadn't seen her for more than ten years. It was probably closer to twelve or more. She might've been around a bit during college breaks, but he couldn't specifically remember seeing her.

"Not really," Claire said, taking her cake and going over and sitting in the rocking chair that was the farthest away from the door. The one by itself.

He figured he could either slide a rocking chair over to her or sit down away from her. He decided he'd sit down on the porch swing, since that was the most comfortable, and it was his favorite spot anyway. If she didn't want to talk to him, he wasn't going to make her.

He'd tried to ask her if there was anything he needed to apologize for, and she'd acted like there wasn't. Except...she'd said "not really."

"'Not really.' Does that mean there is something?"

"No. It's just that seeing you brings back bad memories."

"In what way?" he asked, truly baffled. There was that game of truth or dare, and she had been his first kiss, but...they'd been...eleven? Twelve? Maybe fourteen, but definitely no older. All he knew was it had been nice, and he wouldn't have minded more, but she had acted like it was the grossest thing that had ever happened to her, and he'd ended up embarrassed.

If anyone should have bad memories about that, it should be him, right? Except... It had been his first kiss, and he mostly remembered it with fondness. Although he'd had better kisses over the years, there were none that he remembered with quite so much nostalgia. In fact, if he remembered correctly, it had happened just past the chicken coop in her gram's big barn.

"I don't really want to talk about it," she said, rocking in the chair and not looking at the cake that sat in her lap.

Well, he wasn't going to pass up a piece of homemade cake. His mom's good days were fewer and far between, and she didn't do much baking anymore. Not that chocolate cake was good for him or anything. Still, he took a nice bite and enjoyed the flavor on his tongue as he looked out across the greening pastures.

It had started to get dark, and it was a little chilly. Not so terrible that he felt like he needed to go in, but chilly enough that he was concerned that Claire might be cold, especially if she was just sitting out there because her grandma wanted her to.

"Is there anything you do want to talk about?" he asked, figuring he ought to give the conversation one more try.

She was quiet for a bit, and then she said, "I'm sorry. I know I'm not very good company. I just... There were reasons why I stayed away from here, and seeing you brings a lot of those back."

"I'm sorry about that." He really couldn't help it, though, other than make himself disappear, which he hadn't quite mastered the knack of yet.

"You don't need to apologize. I'm the one that has problems." She didn't look at him as she spoke but glanced down at her cake and then out over the pasture, like there was more to see than the gathering dusk.

"I guess sometimes I feel like it's better to face the things that you don't like than to try to run from them. After all, they always catch up to you one way or another." That's kind of how he'd felt when he'd ended up staying after high school. There were people who thought he was a loser because he wasn't more ambitious, because he didn't go to college, because he still lived with his parents through his twenties and was now in his thirties. There were all kinds of things he could run from, hide from, and try to ignore in his life. But like he had just told Claire, he'd found that sooner or later, they caught up with you.

"I suppose you know all about that," she said, and there was a good bit of sarcasm in her voice.

He didn't say anything. What was he supposed to do? Tell her that he did know about it and start listing all the things he had run from over the years?

He didn't want to do that.

"I suppose I figure that everyone's trial feels big to them. It might not be what someone else is going through. Someone else might have it a lot worse, but in your life, it feels like the biggest thing ever. You know?"

She pressed her lips together. Even from that distance, he could see that they were so tight there was a white line between them.

Whatever he had said had made her mad. It was funny—he was trying to not make her mad but obviously failing miserably.

"Aren't you just a fountain of wisdom," she said, and there was no doubt about the sarcasm in her voice this time.

He put the last piece of cake in his mouth and then chewed slowly.

"You going to eat that?" he asked, nodding at the piece in her lap and figuring that they might not be talking, but he still hated to see a good piece of cake go to waste.

"No," she said softly.

"Mind if I do?" he asked. The cake, at least, was a neutral topic. Unless she got mad at him for wanting the piece she'd just said she wasn't going to eat.

"You ate that whole piece she gave you?" she asked, seeming interested in something about him for the first time since he'd walked in.

"I sure did. I don't get cake very often, so I'm gonna savor every bite and eat as much as I can." That wasn't entirely true. If Miss Mattie tried to shove the entire cake at him, he wouldn't eat it all in one sitting. But since her cake was already cut and she wasn't eating it, he wasn't going to to sit there and pretend he didn't want it.

"I guess I don't," she said, and to his surprise, she got up and walked her plate over, handing it to him.

He took it, holding onto it for just a moment while he looked up, the light still bright enough that he could look into her eyes. "Thank you, ma'am."

"Ma'am. I'm not old enough to be a ma'am." She rolled her eyes and removed her hand from the plate, walking back over to the rocking chair. He half expected her to go back inside.

"Now me being polite has offended you."

"'Ma'am' is for old ladies."

"You're not a young teenager anymore. You're not in your twenties either."

"Don't you know it's impolite to talk about a lady's age?"

"You graduated with me. I know exactly how old you are. Am I supposed to pretend I don't?" he asked before he slid his fork into her cake and put half the piece in his mouth. "Now, if I asked you how much you weigh, you'd have a right to attack me for that."

"I wouldn't attack you." Her head jerked over toward him, and she looked truly offended.

"I don't know. I guess if you say you didn't, then you must not have, but it felt like an attack." Like everything else she'd hurled at him since he'd walked through the door.

"I told you I'm sorry. I guess the move has just been that hard."

"Coming back? To your gram's?" He would have thought that would have been an easy move. Lots of good memories here. For him, anyway. There had to be a few for her at least.

"Yeah."

She didn't elaborate, and he chewed thoughtfully on the cake in his mouth. He swallowed before he said, "I guess I don't understand. To me, there are a few bad memories in our past. A big tragedy, some embarrassing things, like that kiss we shared in the barn." He figured if that was what was bothering her, he might as well get it out in the open.

"Oh my goodness. Are you really going to rub that in?"

"It was my first kiss. I have fond memories of it."

"It was my first kiss too, and I don't have fond memories."

"I think I've gotten better at kissing over the years, but I suppose I shouldn't take offense if I wasn't any good at that point, considering it was my first. I guess you must've just had natural talent."

He'd wondered if it had been her first too. He hadn't thought they were going to talk about that tonight. But there was something that smiled deep inside of him at the thought that they had shared their first kiss. He supposed it should have been something special that he shared with someone who really meant something to him, but at that age, he hadn't exactly been wise or smart or a combination of either one of those things. In fact, he felt like the best word that could describe him would have been stupidly dumb. Hopefully he'd gotten a little better as he'd aged.

She hadn't said anything, and he didn't press her any more on that. "I have so many good memories of this farm. We played hide-and-seek in the barn, we butchered chickens out back, and then your grandma cooked chicken for supper."

"Oh my goodness. That was not a good memory!" Claire said with the first hint of humor in her voice he'd heard the entire time he'd been there. "Talk about wanting to throw up. I don't think anybody ate a bite that night."

"Me either. If you're going to spend your Sunday butchering chickens, eat beef for supper."

She laughed outright at that. It was a little bit of wisdom he'd gleaned from the farm. After spending the day around the stench of chicken, one absolutely could not abide the smell of anything that had to do with cooking chicken.

"All right. You might be right. So that's not a good memory. But everything else is good."

"Maybe for you," she said, and then she didn't elaborate.

"You can't tell me that the bad outweighs the good."

"It just seems bigger somehow. There's more weight to it. More emotional baggage."

"Isn't that in your head?" He was a big believer that a person could control their thoughts. Sure, he could focus on how his mom seemed to get worse and worse every day, how she wasn't cooking hardly at all anymore and hadn't baked in years, how his dad's eyes looked worried when he looked at her, and he didn't know how much longer she'd be with them. Or he could cherish every day that she was there, share laughter whenever they could, and talk about and cherish all the memories of the good times. He supposed it was just a matter of focusing on one or the other, at least for him anyway.

"My thoughts and feelings are part of me. Am I supposed to ignore them?"

"You don't have to ignore them, but you can control them."

"Spoken like a man," she said dismissively.

Glancing over, she saw that he was done with his cake.

"I guess we can go inside. Surely the bread is in the oven by now."

"I can leave. You can tell Miss Mattie that I needed to go. I don't even have to go back inside. My bag's sitting by the door, and I'll just pick it up and I'll be out of here." He really didn't want to make her more uncomfortable than what she obviously already was.

"No. I don't want you to leave because of me. And I'm sure you're looking forward to Grandma's homemade bread just as much as I am. I'm sorry. I need to shake this and not let these things upset me. I guess it's just been a rough year."

He wanted to ask what had made her year rough, but she walked toward the door and moved so he could open it for her to walk in.

Holding both plates in one hand, with his thumb over the forks so they didn't fall off the plates, he carried them in, closing the door behind him and making sure the screen door didn't slam.

Claire didn't look back for him or walk with him into the kitchen. It was like she wanted to make sure there was distance between the two of them. He couldn't blame her for that. Whatever had happened in the last year, whatever she was fighting, whatever had made her feel like the memories from this town were almost unbearable, he felt bad for her. A person needed to get a hold of their thoughts so they didn't allow them to get them down. He supposed she could argue with him if she wanted to, but that was how he had lived, and it had served him well. He wished he could help her do the same.

Four

"And I'm going to have Josiah fix the rose trellis. The rosebush got so heavy it tore it down. That was years ago, and the bush has all but died. I don't know if I can bring it back if I get the trellis fixed or not." Grandma had her cane as she and Claire walked around the old farmhouse.

Claire had taken her children to Blueberry Beach that morning, registered them for school, and they'd gone straight to their classes. She'd come back home and started talking to her grandma about fixing up the old farmhouse. Turns out her grandma already had a plan, and Claire had to admit it was a pretty good one.

The only problem was, she'd be seeing a lot of Josiah McMurtry if Grandma's plan came to fruition.

"Aren't there any other handymen around?" she asked hopefully. She wasn't sure why Josiah brought such bad vibes out in her, but he did. Well, she had a pretty good idea, but she didn't want to examine it too closely. That kiss was one of them—it had been a terrible kiss. Maybe that was the problem. She'd been surprised she'd liked it as much as she had. After all, it was Josiah, and she'd had zero attraction to him. She'd been afraid for a really long time that she was some kind of weird pervert who enjoyed kissing anyone, if she could enjoy kissing Josiah.

And then there was the tragedy. Josiah hadn't been there, and he hadn't been involved, but he had been friends with them and had been affected almost as much as she had.

"Why would I want another handyman?" her grandma asked, sounding aghast. "Josiah is a local guy, honest, and his work is unparalleled."

"Okay," Claire said, seeing that her grandma felt very strongly about it. She doubted she was going to convince her that she shouldn't have Josiah doing anything. And why? Just because Claire didn't have good vibes from him?

She really didn't have good vibes from the idea of meeting anyone in town. And that wasn't anyone else's fault but her own. She'd not been very kind to Josiah, and she'd lain in bed last night thinking about that fact. She owed him a sincere apology, although she'd already apologized a couple of times. She just...wasn't happy to be back, wasn't happy to have her family torn apart.

She loved her grandma and was glad she got to spend time with her, but coming back to Raspberry Ridge had not been an easy thing, and she was struggling with memories. Struggling with the fact that her life hadn't gone the way she'd wanted it to. Struggling with the fact that she was basically coming back a loser.

She hadn't expected to return to town this way. She'd expected to return triumphantly—successful, rich, confident, and the envy of the town. The town's darling, perhaps.

If she ever came back at all. Memories of what had happened here tore at her heart and soul, and she figured Josiah was correct. She was going to need to face them eventually.

There were a lot of ghosts she could run into, and if she ran away from every one of them, she would never be able to show her face in town.

"I appreciate you coming back so much." Her grandma rested her hand on top of her cane and turned to face her fully. "I feel rejuvenated. Like maybe there's a reason for living after all. I suppose I always feel like that after a particularly long, difficult winter. But the older I get, the harder winter is, even when it's really not that bad."

"I'm here now. And I don't have any intention of leaving, unless you kick me out." She wasn't sure whether she could afford it, particularly if her ex didn't continue paying child support, but she'd figure that out when the time came. In the meantime, she had a couple of things she was doing online, including an e-commerce subscription website, which hadn't exactly taken off but gave her a couple hundred dollars of extra income every month.

"I'm not going to kick you out. I'm so happy to have you," her grandma said.

"Tell me more about what you plan to do." She looked at the crumbling old farmhouse. It needed some paint, and she'd like to paint.

"Rather than have Josiah paint the house, why don't I do it?" she said as her grandma mentioned that very thing.

"You?"

"Sure. What else am I going to do around here all day?"

"Well, I did think you'd help me work in the flower beds some, and I'd love to have a big garden, but it's been getting smaller and smaller every year because I just can't keep up with it."

"I can help with the garden and the flower beds and still paint the house. It's not like you have to paint the house in a day. I could spend the entire summer working on it, couldn't I?"

"I suppose so. I really don't know much about painting, though. You'd have to talk to Josiah about it. He's got plenty of experience."

It seemed like her grandma was throwing Josiah at her every chance she got. Or maybe that was just Claire's imagination, exacerbated by the fact that she was trying to avoid having anything to do with Josiah.

"I can talk to him about it. When's he going to be here next?"

"He had a job to do this morning, something at his mom's, and then he was coming here. He'll spend most of his time here, except when he goes and works on the big yachts at Blueberry Beach."

"He works on yachts?" she asked, curious despite herself. Josiah didn't seem like a highbrow kind of guy. He seemed like a humble, sweet hometown kid, the kind that she probably should have married instead of the jerk she'd ended up with. But Josiah had never been attractive to her. She...seemed to be attracted to jerks, much to her dismay.

That was why she had sworn off dating forever. She was just dumb when it came to picking out the man she should spend her life with, and now not only was she suffering, but her kids were suffering too. Someone like her should not be allowed to make their own decisions about the person they were going to spend their life with. Too many people were liable to get hurt.

"Yeah," her grandma said. "That's where he makes most of his money. That's why he's able to work here without charging much of anything at all."

"He doesn't charge you the going rate?"

"I'm not sure what the going rate is, but he charges about half as much as anyone else I've gotten to do any work here. And I only do that if it's an emergency and Josiah isn't available."

She hadn't realized her grandma was so dependent on Josiah. And that Josiah did so much work around the place.

She looked up at the old farmhouse. There was a lot to paint. It wasn't a small house.

But she needed a project like this. Something big, something challenging, something that would keep her mind and body tired enough to sleep at night.

"I'll figure out what I need to do in order to paint it. If I run into something I can't handle, I'm sure Josiah will help me out." He seemed like that kind of guy. The kind of guy who was always kind and eager to help. Well, maybe eager was too strong a word. Ready. He was ready to help. Solid and dependable. He didn't move fast.

He was almost the exact opposite of Ted in every way. Ted was quick, sure, didn't let any grass grow under his feet, and he was more than content to let someone else do the helping while he helped himself.

She thought about that for a little bit and realized there was a lot about Josiah to admire. Maybe it was best that she do the painting and have him there as little as possible. She didn't think there was any danger of her falling for him, but she didn't want to take any chances. She was not going to get married again.

It ended up that Josiah got called out to do some kind of emergency work on a yacht, and he was going to be gone for an entire week. That suited Claire just fine, and in that week, she and her grandma settled into a routine. The kids got up early enough to gather the eggs and feed the chickens before school. One of the kids made breakfast, and her grandma was always there with homemade jelly and to pack lunches for the kids.

Claire was kind of surprised that her kids didn't really mind. Back in Boston, they had never wanted to pack their lunch, but for some reason —maybe it was because other kids took their lunch, because peer pressure was a thing at that age—they seemed to enjoy the fact that Grandma packed their lunch. Claire didn't want to think that maybe Grandma packed a better lunch than she did, but she supposed that was possible. Still, after that, Grandma made coffee and sat down with her Bible while Claire took a walk down the cliff to the beach and spent an hour walking beside the lake while she listened to her Bible through her headphones.

There was something about hearing God's word in one ear and the waves crashing against the shore in the other while the wind lifted her hair off her shoulders and sometimes gusted strong enough to threaten to knock her off her feet.

She loved the lake and the wildness of it, but there was still a nagging feeling that she wanted to get away. She didn't want to get too close, and she never let the water touch her.

Still, after all of that, she worked with her grandma a little bit in the flower beds and the garden, planting onions and peas and spinach and beets and a few other things that grew that early in the spring. And then she started to work on scraping the gable end of the house. She had spent a few evenings googling how to paint a house, and she was fairly certain she would be able to do it. She was going to need scaffolding or else some kind of lift, but she hadn't gotten to that point, and anyone who did it would need that as well, so it wasn't like it was going to be some kind of unexpected expense.

Still, she'd never been very good with heights, and she wasn't entirely sure how she was going to be able to handle being up farther than a few feet. She was determined to do it, though, and so she didn't let herself dwell too much on the idea that it might be more than she could handle.

She didn't want to admit that there was anything she couldn't handle, even though in the recesses of her mind, she knew there were some things. Like a husband who wasn't faithful. Who seduced the therapist, and Claire might not even have known if it hadn't been for the fact that she'd gone in unannounced without an appointment one day, wanting to talk to the therapist alone, since at every session, the therapist seemed to take Ted's side.

After she'd found them on the couch together with their clothes strewn over the chair that the therapist usually sat in, Claire quit having trouble figuring out why everything was always her fault and Ted was the poster child for a husband and father, at least according to their therapist.

Maybe she was a little bitter.

It had been a week since they had moved when her phone rang at about one o'clock in the afternoon. She and Grandma had just finished lunch, and she was working on a ladder, putting off the idea of getting scaffolding or renting a lift, and she'd found that she had been getting comfortable being up a little bit.

Still, she climbed down from the ladder before she pulled her phone out of her pocket and saw her husband's number.

Ex-husband. The divorce had been final for more than eight months.

"Hello?" she said, after debating with herself for a couple more rings as to whether or not she should even answer.

"Claire Bell," he said, and she bit back her irritation.

It had been a cute nickname back when they had been dating and first married. But after he had cheated the first time, it had started to grate on her nerves. Understandably, from what she could tell. Still, they weren't married anymore, and he had no right to mess with her name.

"I've asked you over and over not to call me that." She kept her voice cool, not ice cold, but cool enough to let him know that she wasn't messing around. He liked to charm people, catch them off guard, and take them for everything they had. There was a reason he had become a lawyer.

"Come now. You don't have to be mean."

"What do you need?" she asked, her words clear and containing disinterest. She had no desire to talk to him any longer than she had to.

"I don't know why you have to be so short. After all, we agreed that we were going to stay friends for the children's sake."

"Yes. Friends. Distant friends. Friends who only talk once a year, so you're calling me outside of our yearly conversation. It must be about the children."

She didn't want to be mean. She didn't want to be sarcastic, and she hated that he brought out the worst in her.

"Actually, it is. You said that you were moving to Michigan, but I would still get to see them. When?"

They'd discussed it before she moved. He had wanted her to not be allowed to move out of the state of Massachusetts. But she had not agreed to that as a condition of the divorce. After all, he was the one who had cheated and left and hadn't been able to reconcile despite the therapy they'd tried. Enough said on the therapist. So she'd calmly said that the only place she had to go was Michigan, and somehow they'd figure out a way for him to see the children.

She supposed now was the time to figure that out. Although, if it had been her, they would never figure it out. She didn't want to lose her kids at all, especially to someone who might be teaching them that it's perfectly okay to run around with whatever woman you feel like. And whatever other immoral qualities he wanted to display.

She reminded herself that she needed to be happy that her ex actually wanted to have something to do with her kids. She had a lot of friends whose husbands didn't want to have anything to do with them, especially when they had a new love in their life. She was blessed, and it was better for the kids this way. Even if she hated it. After all, kids would grow up a lot happier if they knew their dad loved them and wanted them.

"What would you like?" she asked, hedging a bit as she walked around the house and sat down on the front porch step.

She had no idea what to offer.

Five

"I think I should get the summer, if you're going to have them during the school year. And I probably should get them at Christmas vacation and Easter too, or spring break, or whatever school districts are calling it now." Ted sounded like he'd thought about it a good bit.

Claire wanted to be thankful that he was a good dad, that he loved her children and wanted to see them, but she really resented right now that he wanted to have anything to do with them. After all, he hadn't wanted to keep their family together enough to actually stop cheating on her and try to make their marriage work. It was hard not to resent that.

"I suppose that sounds fair to me." She didn't like it, didn't want to go three months without seeing her kids, but...that was one of the prices she had to pay for the fact that she'd made a stupid choice and married a jerk. A cheating jerk.

They had set the custody arrangements up before the divorce was final, because the judge had allowed them to. She had wanted to sell their house before she moved, and up until that point, they had been able to have the kids stay with her during school nights and with him on the weekends.

"We'll get the judge to add that to our agreement. I can talk to him tomorrow at work," he said casually.

She might be thinking that he was sleeping with the judge in order to get himself a better deal, but it was a man. So she didn't think so, although her husband was such a scoundrel, she really didn't know what depths he would sink to.

That wasn't fair, and she needed to stop thinking like that.

God loved him, and God wanted her to love him, although she was pretty sure God was okay with her loving him from a distance. She wasn't sure whether Michigan was far enough away from Boston, but it was the best she could do for now.

"All right. I just registered them for school last week, and I'm pretty sure the last day is sometime in May. I'll let you know when I know for sure, and we can make arrangements to get them back to Boston. Do you really want them for the entire summer?" she asked, trying not to sound like she was desperate.

"I think that's fair."

He didn't answer her question. She wanted to press him, but what was the point? The more he thought that she wanted them, the more he would fight to get them for himself, even if he didn't really want them. He would do it just to punish her. But he would do it in such a nice, civilized way that someone not as attuned to his wily ways wouldn't even know that they were being played.

That was her years ago when they'd first met, and she'd fallen for him.

"All right. I'll get back to you on exact dates." She had the papers inside, but she couldn't remember what exactly the school had said. There was a website, and she'd been on it a couple of times, and she could get on it right now if she really wanted to, but she didn't want to while he was on the phone. Was that terrible?

She knew it was, and she wished she was a better person, but she really wasn't.

Movement out of the corner of her eye caught her attention, and she turned, seeing Josiah walking up to the side of the house, his hands in his pockets, his eyes on the work she'd been doing on scraping paint.

Suddenly she wanted to have nothing to do with her ex and to just disappear, although most of her wanted to run out and defend what she was doing to the house. She wanted him to have seen her working and not sitting on the porch talking on the phone.

"Do you need anything else?"

"Why are you whispering?"

Of course he was going to ask that. "No reason. Sorry. Do you need anything else?" She forced herself to talk in a normal tone, although that drew Josiah's attention, and he looked over at her.

She held the phone out from her ear a little bit, and he nodded before looking back at the house.

"No. That was it. Let me know the dates, and I can maybe meet you halfway. That's probably going to be Pennsylvania, although we can figure it out and get an exact spot hammered out at some point."

"All right."

"Thanks for being reasonable."

"Of course," she said, like she'd ever been anything but reasonable. Okay. So there had been a couple of times when she'd screamed at him and thrown a few things, but wasn't that what every woman did when they found out their husband was cheating on them? She supposed she didn't see anything wrong with that. After all, he'd lied to her in a big— a very big—way and destroyed everything she'd been working for for the previous decade and more. She would consider herself crazy if she hadn't wanted to smack him over the head with a cast-iron skillet. Just because she'd thrown a pillow and two slippers at him didn't make her a crazy woman.

They said goodbye and hung up.

She slid her phone back in her pocket and walked over to the ladder, pulling out the scraper she'd shoved in her other pocket and picking up the small propane torch she'd been using to heat the paint so it scraped off easier in her other hand.

"Who's been working on this?" Josiah said before he turned to look at her. Then his eyes fell to the scraper that was in her hand and the propane torch in her other. "Never mind. Guess I have my answer."

"Is that okay with you?" she asked, raising her brows high and acting like she was asking him seriously, like he had any say in it at all. She was emphasizing that, and he got it.

His mouth closed, and his lips pressed together. "Of course. You know I have no say in it. It has to be okay."

"I'm sorry." She wanted to say she was just talking to her ex and was in a bit of a mood, but she didn't want to go into that. Because then she might have to go into more detail, and the last, very last thing she wanted to talk about was her ex. And that wasn't just today, that was any day.

Of course, she was bummed because she knew it was coming, but she hadn't wanted to admit that she probably wasn't going to see her children most of the summer.

Maybe she could sneak in an extra week at the end of the school year and get them back an extra week before the next school year started.

But she wasn't going to try to do that without her ex knowing. That wasn't the way she wanted to be treated, and she couldn't treat him worse than what she expected to be treated by him. That wasn't right, even though she felt like he deserved it. After all, if it wasn't for him, they wouldn't have to figure out how to divide up their kids.

"Do you have some experience in painting houses?" Josiah asked as he examined her work.

Part of her wanted to know what he thought, and part of her wanted to close her ears, because she couldn't stand to be critiqued right now. She already felt like a horrible person. What had been so terrible about her that her husband hadn't been able to stay true? That he would rather be with someone, anyone else, rather than her? That he would break up their entire family in order to get away from her? That he would let her move halfway across the country and not care?

"No. This is my first time, but Google is my friend," she said, trying to lighten the mood and make a little joke.

"She has a sense of humor after all," Josiah said, and somehow the way he said it kept her from taking offense at it. He...wasn't like her ex, where everything was a competition. It was obvious in the casual way he stood and in the interest he showed in her work.

"I have all sorts of hidden talents."

"I'll say. You have a sense of humor, and you can paint houses. Two things I wouldn't have guessed when I first laid eyes on you last week."

"I heard you were working on a million-dollar yacht. I would not have guessed that about you when I first laid eyes on you last week."

"I guess we both have hidden talents," he said.

Suddenly she wondered if maybe he was fooling around with the wife of the owner of one of those million-dollar yachts. Or maybe he didn't bother with the wife—he found yachts where the woman owned it and fooled around with her.

She tried to stop herself. It wasn't fair for her to assign guilt to Josiah. They were very different, as she'd already observed, and Josiah wasn't that kind of person.

Although she would have said Ted wasn't that kind of person either.

"So you really think I'm doing okay?" she asked, hating that vulnerability but needing his reassurance. "I've been kind of worried that I'm ruining my grandma's house."

"No, it looks to me like you're doing it perfectly. Better than I would have done it. Scraping paint is my least favorite job in the world."

"Well, I don't think the fumes are very good for me, but using this little thing has been almost miraculous. I found a video of it on social media and had to try it for myself."

"I can never figure out which thing I need to hold in my dominant hand. I'm a lefty, and I want to hold them both over here, because my right hand is pretty much worthless."

She laughed. "I actually had to juggle that for a little bit too, and it took me a bit to figure out that I wanted the scraper in my right hand, since it's my dominant hand, but I need to be very careful with the torch, because I've burned myself a couple of times." She held her wrist out to show him—there were a couple of red marks, but thankfully she'd had quick enough reflexes that she'd jerked her hand back before it had truly burned her bad.

"Oh boy. Looks like that wasn't too bad, but those things are hot. You be careful."

"I'm definitely trying to be. I would prefer to keep the skin on my hand and not broil it off."

He grinned. "I'm not sure why, but that reminds me that I got some ribs out, and I'm going to make my famous barbecue ribs tomorrow. I'll have to bring you guys some. I take it the kids are in school?"

"They are. And...ribs are my favorite."

When she and Ted went out to a restaurant, she always ordered the ribs. And the waitress almost every single time thought the man was getting the ribs and the woman was getting whatever pasta dish or salad Ted had ordered. They'd always laughed about it.

"Claire?"

"I'm sorry," she said, realizing he had said something, and she had no idea what it was. She'd been lost in the memories. Was that the way it was always going to be? Something would trigger a memory, and she'd remember what she'd lost.

"Nothing important. I just wanted to know if you wanted me to order some scaffolding or a lift. That's what I was planning to use rather than a ladder. It's a little safer."

"I thought I would check and see if I was comfortable above the ground before I spent the money on renting any piece of equipment that was going to get me up higher than my comfort zone."

"And?" he asked, sticking his hand in his pocket and shifting his weight so it was balanced on one foot with a hip stuck out. It was a casual pose, and for some reason, she noticed the ripple of muscle under his T-shirt.

She jerked her eyes away. "And I haven't gotten dizzy or fallen off, and I've been okay. But I've only made it up to the third rung. It's going to take a lot longer than what I was thinking to paint this house."

The first day she'd done it, she'd gone to bed with aching muscles and woken up with arms that were so sore she wasn't sure she would be able to use them that day. But the more she'd used them, the more they'd limbered up, and her grandma had told her to drink a lot of water. She supposed that had helped, because she almost couldn't feel it anymore, and she thought she might be developing some muscles of her own. Before she knew it, she was going to look like a bodybuilder.

"House painting is not for the faint of heart. Although spraying it on is actually kind of fun."

"You're not using a paintbrush?"

"No way. Paintbrushes are for the previous generation. Us modern guys use sprayers all the way."

She lifted her brows and then laughed.

"Seriously, paintbrushes are good for some things, but if you've got a lot of area, a sprayer is the way to go. You can waste a lot of paint. If you're just doing something like a rocking chair or piece of furniture, or even the porch, it's okay. But when you're doing something as big as a house, a sprayer makes it worth it."

"I'll keep that in mind. Although, are you trying to take over?" She wasn't sure whether she resented that or not. Did she want help? Or did she want to do this by herself?

"I suppose it's up to you. Miss Mattie gave me a whole list of things she wanted me to do, and this is on it. I can help you, or I can check this off my list and go work on something else."

She thought about it for a minute. What else was she going to do all summer while her kids were gone?

"Can I work on it myself, and if it turns out to be too big of a job, I'll ask you to help?" She tilted her head to the side. "That's pretty much what I told Grandma I was going to do. I would try, but if I needed you, I wouldn't hesitate to ask."

"I'm happy to hear that. After the way we started off the last time I was here, I kinda thought that maybe you would go out of your way to avoid talking to me."

He had an intense look on his face, like he was studying her for her reaction. She felt her cheeks heating.

"I'm sorry. There is no excuse for my behavior. Then or today. I... I could say that I've been going through a hard time, an emotional time, but that's no excuse not to be nice to people. Kindness is a command in the Bible, and to not be kind is just as bad of a sin as any of the sins that we would say would be terrible."

Including adultery. How could she point fingers at her husband and think about what a terrible person he was, when she allowed herself to not be kind? It was so easy to think someone else's sin was worse than one's own.

"That's an interesting take. One that I hadn't really thought about. But I suppose the Bible does say that sin is sin, and not to do something that you know you should do is a sin, just as much as doing something that you know you shouldn't."

"Exactly." It's what she'd been telling herself and part of the reason she was actually able to talk civilly to her husband. Ex-husband. After all, she wanted to take the moral high ground and say that she hadn't cheated, and so therefore she wasn't as bad as he was. But she hadn't been kind. There'd been the fact that she had thrown the pillow and two slippers at him, and that had not been kind either. Even though she wanted to justify that, still, it was sin.

She turned back toward the house, not really thinking about it but realizing that was more than she wanted to get into with Josiah. How had she started talking to him in the first place? She didn't even like him. And didn't want to be friends.

Except it seemed like that would be inevitable if he was going to be around.

"All right. I'll let you get to it. I have a list of other things your grandma wants me to do, so I'll go start with the flower boxes. I've got a feeling she's going to be ready to put flowers in soon."

"I can't wait. That's how my memories of this house are—with it overflowing with loads and loads of blooming, beautiful flowers." She was sharing more than she should have. Wasn't she just thinking that she didn't want to share with him? And yet... He was so easy to talk to.

"We'll do our best to make sure that's the way it looks this summer."

She didn't talk to him about the kids. What was the point of having a beautiful house all summer if she didn't have her children here to enjoy it?

The idea of moving back to Boston, trying to find a place and a job and... What would be the point of that? She'd have to work so much she'd barely see her kids all summer anyway. Then she'd have to try to find someone to watch them.

She hated this. Hated the fact that her husband had forced her into this position. This wasn't what she'd wanted for her life. Why did she have to suffer because her husband couldn't keep his word?

But even if she had her kids all the time, she didn't have a husband and family, a mom and dad to raise the kids the way they were supposed to be raised. Children didn't thrive in one-parent homes. They just didn't. The best place for a child was in a home with both biological parents.

She sighed, knowing that there was nothing she could do about that. She couldn't fix her husband, she couldn't change the past, and all she could do was try to make the best of everything going forward. She hated what had happened, but she was left with no other choice.

Putting a foot on the ladder, she started to climb.

"Hey, Mom. You're up." Josiah walked into the kitchen as evening descended along the lakeshore.

His mom, recovering from her MS flare-up, typically was in bed when he got home.

"I'm feeling a little better. And I wanted to fix supper for you."

His dad was staying overnight in Blueberry Beach. He worked three long days, then a short day, and was home the other three.

On the days when his dad worked, he tried to make a point of being around for his mom. Time had gotten away from him this evening. Maybe because of talking to Claire, of realizing that she'd become a different, better person than she had been in school, or maybe just wanting, for some strange reason, to get the work done at the house so she could enjoy the flowers she'd talked about with such love and fondness.

He was a fool. She wasn't going to care whether he got the house done fast or slow. But for some reason, he was driven to do it.

"Thanks. It's always nice to come home to someone to talk to," he said. Sometimes he liked to be alone with his thoughts, but he knew that his mom most likely was not going to be around for decades, and he had made a vow when she had first been diagnosed with MS that he would appreciate every second he had with her. He hadn't always been able to keep that vow, but he kept trying.

"I didn't realize you were lonely," she said, walking slowly to the cupboard to get out a bowl so she could scoop out the soup he'd made the night before, when he'd gotten home from working on the yachts.

He tried to make his work schedule when he had to be away align with his dad's work schedule when he got to be home. They didn't always make it happen, and they had a neighbor lady who could come and help with his mom. Still, he liked it best when he or his dad was able to take care of her.

"Mom, you don't have to do that. I can get it warmed up, and you can sit here and talk to me."

"I like to take care of people. I know it's ironic, saying that when I need so much care myself. But let me, since I'm feeling well enough today."

He nodded, grabbed a spoon from the drawer and iced tea from the fridge, and poured himself a glass before sitting down at the small kitchen table.

There was no need to go into the dining room and sit there, with it only being his mom and him. They were very casual when his dad wasn't around.

"How's Miss Mattie doing?" his mom asked.

He paused. He'd told her that Miss Mattie had been diagnosed with leukemia about six months prior, and her prognosis. He had wondered each time he was there whether Claire knew or not. She didn't act like she did. He didn't know if she'd be wasting her time working on a ladder painting a house if she knew. He wished that Miss Mattie would tell her, and then she could make the decision that he had made years ago regarding his mother.

"She's doing well. Can't really even tell," he said as his mother nodded and the microwave beeped, and she walked slowly over to get his bowl.

She set the steaming soup in front of him and then walked to the refrigerator to grab butter before she pulled bread off the counter.

He remembered the smell of warm baking bread that had drifted out of the house while he was working, and he had wondered if Claire had had a hand in it. Miss Mattie was known for her delicious homemade bread, and it would be a shame if Claire didn't learn how to make it too.

But no one had asked him, and he needed to keep his opinions and thoughts to himself, although...

"I told you her granddaughter and her two children have moved in with Miss Mattie?"

"You did. Claire. I remember her from your school days."

Their school wasn't that big, and neither was the town. Everyone knew everyone else. So it didn't surprise him that his mom remembered her.

"I don't think she told Claire about her diagnosis. I'm not sure if I should say anything or not." He was hoping his mom might have some words of wisdom.

She paused, setting the salt and pepper down in front of him before she sank into the other chair. "I don't know what to say about that. I know Claire would want to know, but I also think that if Miss Mattie wanted her to know, she would tell her. So you're torn, because they want different things, most likely."

Yeah. That was the problem. He nodded and then said grace before starting to eat. "Did you already eat?"

"I wasn't very hungry tonight," his mother said.

He tried not to worry about that. He wasn't going to try to coax her to eat if she wasn't hungry. Although if she was hungry and just too tired to make something, he would do his best to help her. But that didn't seem to be the case—she'd just warmed soup up for him.

"I never thought when you were a teenage boy that you'd be able to make soup that tastes that good. I had some earlier."

Maybe that was why she wasn't hungry. He shoved the thoughts away. He'd long ago accepted that she was going to have good days and bad days, and she wasn't going to get better. MS wasn't a disease that could be cured. So bad days were to be expected. Not that he liked it, but he couldn't let himself go into a tailspin every time it seemed like she wasn't doing as well as he wanted her to.

"I'm glad you liked it." He didn't mention that he'd had to learn to cook for survival reasons, since she was often sick and in bed, and if he wanted to eat, he had to figure out something to make himself. Plus, he was responsible for taking care of his mom. That was part of the reason he'd stayed home and didn't move out of the town or the house he'd grown up in. He could hardly take care of her if she starved to death under his watch.

But there was no need to say any of that. His mom already knew it, and him saying it would just make her feel bad because she felt like it was her responsibility to take care of him. And she had always been very nurturing—she loved taking care of other people, and it was hard for her to sit and let others take care of her.

Everyone had a cross, he supposed. Some people had to learn to do things they hated, and others had to learn to be still and let others help, even when it was hard.

"I seem to recall you had a little crush on Claire when you were younger," his mom said casually, like she was just making conversation and not accusing him of having a crush all of his life and still having it.

He tried not to take offense, and then he wondered why he would. Surely he could talk about someone he'd had a crush on when he was in junior high. But it made him uncomfortable... Did he still have feelings for her?

Had he carried them all the way from junior high, and seeing her again, remembering how she was... He supposed he'd always admired her. From a distance in their friend group, since she wasn't interested in him in the slightest. Still wasn't. And he supposed that was something he needed to remember so he didn't go mooning over someone who wasn't interested in him and never would be. But he thought they could be friends.

"She was my first kiss," he told his mom, wondering if that was something boys were supposed to talk to their mothers about. Maybe if his mom wasn't sick, maybe if she were able to have a normal life, he wouldn't talk to her about those things. But she couldn't really go out and have lunch with her girlfriends very easily. As her disease progressed, she was able to do less and less.

"My goodness. Where was that?"

"In Miss Mattie's barn. We played truth or dare, and she got stuck with being dared to kiss me. I forget how we were playing it, but I wasn't too upset about it, though I think she was grossed out."

"Well, sometimes teenage boys aren't very appealing, and then they grow into themselves. Maybe she'll notice that you've changed a good bit since you were a teenager."

"I don't think she's interested in someone like me. She was married to a high-dollar lawyer in Boston, from what I understand." He'd heard that from his mom, so he knew she knew it too.

"She's not married to him anymore. There are reasons for that. Maybe she's looking for something different."

"Maybe I'm not looking for anything at all. Maybe I'm happy where I'm at. Maybe I'm not interested in the problems that come with being with someone who is divorced, with children, and all that baggage."

It would be a lot of drama. And his mother and her illness was all the drama he could handle. Sometimes it was more—it felt like that anyway—even though he knew that God would never give him anything God wasn't going to help him through.

And God could do anything.

"Maybe the drama of a wife, one with baggage or without, is what a man needs in order to grow and mature. Maybe that's part of what makes him a man—dealing with all the trials that a woman brings into his life."

"I suppose," he said, although he'd never really thought about that before. It could be true. After all, dealing with people, learning how to get along with them, to love them despite their faults, to be patient with them when they didn't live up to expectations, or when they fell into sin that he thought should be easily avoided, or just habits and flaws that irritated him—all of that helped him become a better person. He supposed his mother was right about that. What could be more helpful than having to live with someone who was just as big a sinner as he was, only in different areas? And who had just as many faults and flaws as he did, only in areas that irritated him.

"And I wouldn't blame her for the baggage. Sometimes people can't help it that they end up with stuff. Now, sometimes it's our own fault that we get saddled with things, because we've made stupid decisions, but sometimes a man leaves a woman and it's not really her fault at all. It's just because he didn't have the character to keep his word and stay."

"You're blaming the man an awful lot, don't you think? It goes both ways. It could be the man who's saddled with baggage because the woman he married didn't have character or enough integrity to do what she said she was going to do."

He was teasing his mom just a little bit, but he was also serious. It seemed like the world was so eager to blame men, and it was irritating sometimes, because it was almost like women got a free pass and men paid for everything. He did believe that a man should be a protector and provider, but he also believed that a man shouldn't take the blame for the sins of womankind.

"Of course. I'm sorry. You're right. I was blaming men, but that was because I was talking to you, a man, and we were talking about Claire, and I was just saying it may not be her fault." She let out a little laugh. It sounded tired, and he thought maybe he should stop the conversation. But his mom continued to talk. "Of course, I could be taking Claire's side in this, and maybe her divorce was all Claire's fault. Maybe she ran off with a man who ditched her, and her husband wouldn't take her back."

"Somehow I doubt Claire's really that type." He pictured her standing beside the paint she'd already scraped off, her hands on her hips, her eyes going up the side of the house, trying to figure out whether she was going to be brave enough to stand on some kind of scaffolding or lift and scrape the higher parts.

She'd had her chin jutted out and her eyes narrowed, and he'd be willing to bet she got it done. He admired that kind of grit and didn't really think that was the kind of person who'd run off with a man and wreck her family.

But he'd been wrong about a lot more than a woman's character before.

"I didn't think she was that type either."

His mother smiled, and he got the feeling that she had really liked Claire, maybe still did, although she didn't know her.

"Does she know she was your first kiss?" she asked.

"I told her a couple of days ago. I found out that I was her first kiss too." He laughed a little to himself and did not share with his mom that he had been more impressed with her initial kissing abilities than she had been with his. In fact, he'd gotten the feeling that she had been kind of grossed out by him.

It didn't make him feel very good about himself, because it wasn't like he'd done a lot of practicing between then and now. Some, but not much. Not much at all, since he didn't see the point in kissing women he didn't plan on marrying. And while short-term pleasure was tempting, he had never been the kind of person who had trouble looking at the long-term goals he wanted to achieve in his life. Kissing every woman in the county was not one of those. In fact, he didn't want his wife to have to walk down the street and wonder which women they passed were women he had kissed.

Claire was in a select group, although it apparently wasn't a group to be proud of, at least not in Claire's opinion.

"If you don't mind, I'm going to head upstairs to bed. My legs are aching, and my back hurts too."

"I don't mind at all. I'll check on you before I go to bed, okay?"

"You don't have to go to bed early because of me."

"I want to get an early start in the morning, and I have a good book I've been reading. It's upstairs, so I might as well stay up there."

Normally he might sit on the porch for a little bit, if it wasn't chilly, as it often was in the spring. Still, the promise of summer was heavy and ripe in the air, and the idea that he would be spending a lot of it with Claire made him feel brighter. Except...was she going to get a job? What was she going to do? Were her kids going to be there all summer?

He was curious, wanted to know, and that was kind of unusual. Usually he could just take things as they came.

He got up, rinsing out his dish before putting it in the dishwasher and putting the soup away. He thought they had enough to last through tomorrow, when he was going to make ribs.

Was this what his life was going to consist of? Taking care of his mom when his dad wasn't home, cooking for her, and thinking about the girl with whom he'd shared his first kiss?

Maybe the anticipation in the air wasn't because of summer coming. Maybe it was because of something else. Like his life was going to shift in a major way.

He shook his head. That was silly.

Seven

"It always helps when the kitchen is warm. In the winter, it's harder to get your bread to rise, and you have to wait longer. Come summer, it'll rise so fast it'll practically fly out of the pan, and you'll have to chase it across the kitchen floor."

Claire laughed at her gram's exaggeration.

There really wasn't a whole lot to making bread, but somehow her grandma had a knack for making it better than anyone she knew, and she was hoping to learn it herself. Her grandma had agreed to teach her, and Claire had already had several not-so-good failures.

The bread tasted okay, but it didn't have that light, sweet, yummy taste and soft texture that her gram's bread had.

Grandma explained that it really had to do with kneading it, but Claire didn't understand what she was doing differently than what her grandma did. She did everything her grandma told her to.

Grandma said it just took time.

"All right. I'm going to take my walk by the lake while this rises."

"That's good. I'll do my devotions in my chair."

They smiled at each other—a little change in their routine—as the bread lesson had taken a little extra time that morning.

Her kids were going to be sick of homemade bread by the time she was done, because they'd had it every night for supper for the last three nights. And it hadn't been fabulous. But she'd made garlic bread, and then grilled cheese sandwiches, and Grandma had made some kind of vegetable soup that had gone perfectly with it the third night.

They'd just have to figure out something to have with it tonight. But she'd think about that while she was walking.

She opened the door and came face-to-face with Josiah. How could she have forgotten about him? He'd been there all three days as well.

She was starting to get used to him. A little, anyway.

"Good morning," he said from where he was on his knees in front of the flower beds in front of the house.

"Good morning. I don't know why I forgot you were going to be here this morning," she said, feeling silly for startling when she'd seen a man kneeling as she'd opened the door.

"You had a lot on your mind."

"Yeah, I guess I did." Making bread, mostly. Because she didn't want to think about any of the other hard things. Including the fact that she knew exactly when school ended for the year, and she still hadn't sent her husband the date. Nor had she tried to figure out a route where they could find the best place for them to meet and exchange the kids.

It was the fact that she dreaded exchanging the kids and losing them for the entire summer that was making her reluctant, she was sure.

"What's the matter? You look down today."

Did she? She didn't mean to. She brightened her expression and tried to put on a smile. "Sorry." She finished walking out the door, closing it carefully behind her without allowing the screen door to slam.

"That's fine. Don't tell me." He paused. "I was just talking to my mom last night, and her MS is getting worse."

"I didn't realize your mom had MS."

"She was diagnosed when I was still in high school. But there's been a big change in what docs are able to do since then."

"I'm so sorry. That must be really hard to have something that you know you're never going to get rid of."

"She has such a great attitude. She hardly ever gets down. Not being able to do things, to serve people, is probably the hardest thing for her."

"I remember her as always being a mom who volunteered to help in class." That probably hadn't helped make Josiah more likable in her eyes. After all, when kids were in school, their goal was to avoid parents, right? And if someone's parents were in there all the time, especially if they acted like they liked their parents, as Josiah had seemed to, that kind of made him a pariah to the rest of the kids.

"Yeah. She loved that. I think she wished she would have had a whole pile more kids and become a teacher. That was just her jam—all those kids that needed help."

"Her cookies were the best," Claire said honestly. She still remembered Mrs. McMurtry's cookies.

"She hasn't made cookies in years. A lot of times, she doesn't even cook a meal. Putting a sandwich together is too hard for her, although she was able to heat soup up for me the other day."

"Wow. That must be really hard for you."

"I'm just determined that I'm going to cherish every day with her." He lifted his shoulder, leaning back on his haunches and putting his hands on his thighs. "There isn't anything more you can do, especially with something like that."

"Yeah. Well, that's a good attitude. I suppose I was just thinking that sometimes things happen that we don't like, and if we can't change them, we have to learn to somehow accept them and live with them. That's what I was thinking about when I came out—the fact that my kids have to go back to Boston for the summer to be with their dad and I don't want them to."

"Ouch."

"I know. I'm supposed to let my husband know when the last day of school is so we can arrange a time to meet and exchange them. And then I'll pick them up right before school starts. I wish I had a little bit of the summer to spend with them."

"Why don't you see if he'll let you keep them for a week after they get out and bring them back a week before they go back? That way, you get two weeks, and he gets everything else."

Claire stared at him. She had considered that. She'd also thought about asking for a week in July or something, since he got all the holidays during school, but that would mean a two-day trip out and a two-day trip back, and that would be most of the week. She'd figured the kids probably wouldn't want to spend that much time driving unless she could have them longer. Of course, she'd thought about flying, but that was expensive, and while the kids could fly by themselves, she didn't really want to send them on a plane alone.

"I didn't think about that. That makes me feel a little bit better. Like we have a little bit of time to decompress and then to gear back up before school starts, instead of getting them and giving them away as soon as school's out, and getting them the day before they have to go back. I should ask about that." She shook her head. Maybe she was just so gloom and doom that her brain just couldn't come up with solutions. "Thanks." She tilted her head.

"I think I've been smelling a lot of fresh bread in the house lately. I'll accept your thanks in the form of a warm slice or two with melting butter." He gave her a grin and then leaned back over the flower beds, adjusting the border that had slipped and was crooked.

"I have to think about that," she said, knowing that she would give him as much fresh homemade bread as he wanted. "Are you going to be here for lunch?" He seemed to leave during lunchtime, and her grandma had said that he went home to eat with his mom a lot when he was around and close by and his dad wasn't there.

"I will. Dad's home, and he'll be with Mom today. So I can skip lunch at home and eat fresh homemade bread with melted butter to my heart's content."

"All right. I just put dough back to rise, so unless I screwed up, you should have plenty of bread to eat to your heart's content."

He grinned at her but didn't stop working. Just nodded his head.

She smiled and found herself still smiling after she had walked down the steps and started away from the house. Why did she feel lighter than she had in a long time? Was it just talking to Josiah? Or was it figuring out a solution to a problem that had been bothering her? Or not dreading talking to her husband so much? She was almost certain he would give her those two weeks, especially when she reminded him that he was getting Christmas break and Easter, and she would like to have the Fourth of July. But instead of making the kids do an extra trip, she would just take the extra time at the end of the year and the extra time at the beginning.

It was a perfect compromise.

She found herself humming a bit as she went down the steep hill to the lakeshore.

Was she really that happy? Had the short time she'd been at her grandma's house really changed her outlook that much?

She knew it had. She'd fallen into a routine, one that she loved. Walking along the lake every morning, working on scraping the paint from the house after she got back, helping her grandma with anything that she needed, and spending time in the evening with her grandmother and kids in the living room, doing homework and reading books and doing family things. Sure, she missed the idea of having a husband and a dad for her children in the home, but she did really love how things had worked out.

Maybe she wasn't completely happy, but she'd definitely taken steps in the right direction.

As she started along the beach, she saw two horses in the distance. That had to be Becky and Rodney, people who had moved into Raspberry Ridge and gotten married since she'd moved away.

She'd talked to them a little bit, but today they just rode by, waving from the top of their big Clydesdales. Apparently, they had carriage rides they rented out during the tourist season. They had a presence down the beach and got most of their business from there. But they were hopeful that Raspberry Ridge would start to see some of the overflow.

Claire wasn't sure exactly how she felt about that. On the one hand, eggs and home-baked bread might be nice things to sell to the tourists, but she also loved how quaint and quiet and almost unchanged Raspberry Ridge was from when she was younger. Other than the healing garden, which was a definite asset, most of the town had stayed the same. Tourists would change all that.

But tourists would also give people business and keep them from needing to move out of town.

She looked up at the hill—just barely visible in the distance was the old Lakeside Inn. Maybe someone would even reopen it.

She could imagine how derelict it was, since it had looked old and run-down when she was a kid. Maybe someone would just bulldoze it down, and the idea of reopening it was a pipe dream.

For some reason, she thought about Josiah and her, how they were helping to fix up Grandma's old farmhouse.

Maybe they could buy the inn and... Wait. Was she trying to think of things for her and Josiah to do together? What was wrong with her?

She pulled her earbuds out of her pocket and stuck them in her ears. Normally she listened to her Bible while she walked, but she'd had so much on her mind, she'd started out without them. She needed to empty her mind of all her worldly thoughts and cares and fill it with God's word. That had been the best start to her day she could have imagined. Maybe that was the reason everything seemed to be shifting into a more positive mindset.

Eight

"This smells amazing," Josiah said as he walked into the kitchen, his nose in the air, smelling fresh, warm, homemade bread. It was not quite noon, and the bread was done. Claire had said they might as well go in and eat.

He was all over that. He had made breakfast for himself this morning—fried eggs with a few vegetables thrown in. He supposed most people would call it an omelet, but he didn't get fancy with it. His mom hadn't had anything—she hadn't been hungry. He'd reminded her that there was yogurt and fruit in the fridge before he left.

His dad was home, and it wasn't his problem. Not really, although it was his mother, so he would always care, even if he wasn't necessarily obligated to be the one who took care of her.

"As I recall, I owe you at least two pieces," Claire said. She'd warmed up to him, and he appreciated the fact that she smiled a friendly smile as she turned around with two thick, crusty pieces of bread with big slabs of butter melting on top of each.

"I don't think I need anything else for lunch other than this," he said, grinning at her and then smiling at Miss Mattie.

She looked tired, and he noted several bruises on her arms. It was funny that Claire hadn't seemed to notice, or maybe she had and Miss

Mattie had brushed them off. Still, Claire did not seem the slightest bit worried.

"Miss Mattie, come sit down. I can do whatever it is you're doing."

"You will not. You're taking care of your mom. When you're here, we take care of you."

He did not miss the fact that Claire rolled her eyes behind her grandmother's back. Then she saw him looking at her, and she looked a little bit embarrassed but did not duck her head.

Instead, she shrugged her shoulders a little bit like "whatever."

Yeah, she didn't particularly like "taking care" of him. And he couldn't say that he blamed her. They were practically strangers. Just because he enjoyed talking to her when they worked outside together didn't mean anything.

Finally, Miss Mattie sat down in a chair, and she seemed to do it gingerly, like her joints were aching too.

Claire seemed to be chalking everything up to Grandma getting older. She'd mentioned something along those lines a couple of times with him.

"Will you say grace for us?" Miss Mattie asked, looking to Josiah where he sat at the head of the table. That was where she had always put his plate, and it had become "his" seat when he was at Miss Mattie's house. He sat here now without thinking, but maybe Claire resented him sitting at the head of the table at the house where she lived.

He didn't really care one way or the other. He wasn't the kind of guy who needed to be the head of everything. But he also wasn't going to let a woman rule him. He didn't see that in the Bible anywhere, other than as a sign of weakness in a man and a sign that there were no brave men to step up, so God had to use a woman.

Women could do it—it just wasn't God's plan.

He prayed and then used his knife to spread butter out on the bread.

Still warm and soft, and probably his favorite thing to eat in the world.

He bit into it and immediately knew that it was not Miss Mattie's bread.

It was coarser in texture, wasn't nearly as soft and fine, but...the taste was the same, and he closed his eyes as the warm butter oozed over his tongue, mixing with the yeasty bread and creating an experience that was only possible to have in a farmhouse kitchen, sitting around the big table, with someone who had taken the time to make bread from scratch.

He wasn't oblivious to the fact that not everyone in modern society got to experience this. It made it all the more precious.

"You're making me feel like maybe my bread isn't as bad as what I think it is." Claire's words broke into his enjoyment.

They didn't detract from it, though.

He opened his eyes. "I'm acting a little strange, aren't I? Maybe I should stop moaning at the dinner table and just go eat outside on the porch."

They laughed. "It's not that bad," Claire assured him.

After she'd rolled her eyes at the idea of taking care of him, he wasn't sure that she actually meant it, but he wasn't going to hold it against her. Whatever she felt for him, he couldn't help it. It didn't make it any easier that every time he was around her, he admired her a little more. She was funny and truly wanted to master the bread, and the grit that she displayed as she continued to scrape the paint off the side of the house was inspiring as well. She had allowed him to order a lift for her, and she had figured out how to use it, and now she was almost up to the second story with it. Yeah, he thought she was going to do it, and he didn't tell her, but he was rooting for her.

"I don't know how long it's going to take you with the other projects, but with Claire in here using the kitchen, I was thinking that it might be nice to do a total kitchen makeover. I've been looking at prices online and getting ideas as well. Is that something you might be interested in?" Miss Mattie said, surprising him.

"That's a pretty big project, but I'm sure I can do it. I might need a little help with lifting some of the heavier things, like putting the cabinets up and stuff." He usually worked alone, but there had been multiple times when he'd wished for a partner. Someone to help him with lifting heavy things or giving him a hand on a rush job on a yacht. A lot of times, the highbrow owners wanted impossible work done in an impossible amount of time. A partner would make the impossible

possible some of the time. Sometimes there just wasn't anything anybody could do to do what the owners wanted.

But he didn't complain, because those jobs were what contributed to the nest egg he was saving. Since he didn't have to pay for room and board and didn't have a mortgage or rent to pay.

He figured someday his parents would be gone, and... He didn't know what he would do then, but it wouldn't hurt to have some money stashed away.

"Maybe before you go back out, I can show you some of the things I was thinking about, to make sure. And then we'll have to figure out what we need to order."

"All right. I've got all the time you need. As long as the bread keeps coming, I'll sit here and not move a muscle. You can show me anything. Even purses."

"Oh. Purses? I didn't realize you were interested in those," Claire teased him, and it was his turn to roll his eyes. He didn't figure he was probably as good at it as Claire was, and he was guessing he probably didn't have as much practice. After all, he was an adult, and adults were supposed to have outgrown the proclivity toward eye rolls, right?

Still, Claire laughed, and he thought she got his joke.

It was fun to share a little bit of wordless interplay and laugh about it.

He had to turn away. He didn't want to have those feelings toward someone who could barely stand to look at him and would prefer that he not be in her house at all, if she had any say in it.

It was over an hour before Miss Mattie was done showing him all the things she wanted to show him on her computer. He had her email him a few links and told her he'd work up a price for her in the next few days.

By that time, both loaves of bread were gone, and they truly hadn't had anything else to eat for lunch. He figured he would probably be hungry in the middle of the afternoon since there hadn't been any protein at the meal, although the butter he'd consumed would probably keep him full a little bit longer. And it was worth it, just to have that warm homemade bread.

"You do really well with my grandma," Claire said as they walked outside the front door together. She could have gone around the side—it would be closer for her—but she seemed to be in a talking mood.

"What did you think of her kitchen?" he asked, not knowing what to say about her compliment. Thank you? That was the only thing that came to mind. After all, he wasn't trying to be good with her grandma. He just liked Grandma and enjoyed spending time with her and enjoyed talking to her, and he supposed that came out in their interactions. It wasn't something that was contrived. But he didn't want to lecture Claire about that. She probably knew it anyway.

"I liked it. She and I had looked at some things previously, but I didn't really think that she was going to have it done so quickly."

He thought about the issues that Grandma had and wondered if the kitchen would even be done before she passed away. He'd looked leukemia up online, but most of it talked about treatment and life expectancy and that type of thing if someone were going to a doctor. Since Miss Mattie had chosen to not be treated, he wasn't sure where that put her.

"Did she seem like she was extra tired to you?" Claire said as they stepped off the bottom of the front porch steps. She sounded like she hadn't really wanted to ask him, but the question came out anyway. Now she tilted her head and studied him, her eyes narrowed as though she were running over all the things in her mind that had hit her and just wanted him to reassure her that Grandma was fine.

What was he supposed to do? He couldn't lie. But he didn't want to tell her what was going on with her grandmother if Miss Mattie hadn't said something herself. After all, if Miss Mattie hadn't told her, there must've been a reason for it.

"Well, I suppose she does seem more tired than she used to be." Even from this winter, when she was first diagnosed. Definitely from last summer, when she had been much more spry, still smiling and energetic, although obviously older.

"That's how I feel too. A lot more tired than what she should be. I think I'm going to say something to her about going to the doctor. I... I don't want to borrow trouble, but my gut tells me there's something wrong."

"Maybe you should see if she would go," he said, knowing that

Claire was going to be mad when she found out that he knew and didn't tell her. She might not understand that he wasn't going to spout off knowledge that wasn't his to share.

"Did you see those big bruises on her arms?" Claire started to take a step away but turned around and shot that question out.

"I saw them while we were talking, yeah."

"She told me she didn't know what she did to cause them."

"I guess that happens sometimes," he said, knowing that bruising was one of the symptoms of leukemia that he'd read about.

"But big bruises like that. You'd think that she would remember, wouldn't you?" She paused and then continued before he could answer her. It was a good thing, since he really didn't know what to say. "I guess part of me wonders whether she's losing her mind too. She...seems like she's all there, but then something like that happens, and I know that she should remember what happened, but she claims not to. I just... I have so many other things on my mind right now, I don't know if I can handle anything happening to my grandma."

"If something happens to her, God's with you. He's not going to give you more than what He will help you handle."

"That's not helpful," she said, leveling her gaze at him and not smiling.

He didn't figure it would be. People knew it, but they insisted on worrying anyway. "I'll be here to help. Although that might not be any more helpful."

"I guess it should be. I should be happier about God being with me than you, but... You're starting to feel like an anchor. Thank you." She paused for a moment, and then she added, "I'm sorry I rolled my eyes. It wasn't necessarily at you—it was at the idea that she was volunteering my services and—"

He waved a hand. "Don't worry about it. It wasn't annoying. I got that anyway, and—"

She laughed. "I saw."

He knew she had, and they laughed about it, which was what he wanted. He didn't want silent wars behind Miss Mattie's back where the two of them couldn't get along. He wasn't going to take offense at anything she did. He was just going to make up his mind that he was going to get along. If she chose not to, she'd have a hard time fighting with someone who had already decided they weren't going to fight. Now, if he could only live that out somehow.

"I guess just talking to you somehow made me feel better. Thanks," she said as she turned around and started walking away again, disappearing around the corner of the house.

He had the flower beds mostly fixed, although the ones alongside the house needed to have new weed fabric put down. He was going to wait until after Claire was done scraping the paint off that side before he got into a job like that.

The railing on the back porch needed to be fixed, and that would be a job he could finish before he went home today.

Thinking it was funny that maybe he and Claire were going to be friends after all, he found himself whistling as he stepped off the walk and followed her around the house.

Nine

Grandma was on Claire's mind the next week as she started her normal morning walk along the lake. As she stepped onto the path that took her down around the cliff, her phone buzzed, and she looked to see a text from her ex.

She wanted to slap herself. She'd talked to Josiah about adding an extra week after school and adding an extra week before school started, but she had totally forgotten to message her ex about it and see what he thought.

Now, this text did not sound happy.

> Are you ignoring me? When does school
> end? Do we need to do this through the
> courts?

He was a lawyer, and part of the reason she really didn't want to go through the courts was because he knew most of the judges. He knew the judge who would be handling their case, and she thought he might get special treatment.

He was so good at charming people, and that judge didn't seem immune to his charms. In fact, she wouldn't be surprised if that was one of the people he had cheated with. He really liked appearing before that judge.

He'd made no bones about that during their marriage, although it hadn't been until the last year or so that Claire had realized what the reason for that might be.

She held her phone in her hand for a moment and thought about what she should say. She didn't want to appear too conciliatory or like she was begging him to forgive her. But at the same time, it was an honest mistake.

She figured an apology wouldn't show too much weakness, although Ted was very attuned to attacking a person at their weakest point. It was a lawyer thing, she was pretty sure.

She reprimanded herself. Just because Ted was a terrible person didn't mean all lawyers were bad. Still, she knew she was going to have trouble believing that for a long time to come.

> I'm sorry. I totally forgot. The last day of school is May 17. I was wondering if you might be okay if the kids stayed with me for an extra week after school ends and came back a week before school begins? I thought of doing this rather than having them over for the July 4th holiday in the middle of the summer. That will save them the long, two-day trip from here to there. It seemed fair, since you get them for all the holidays during the school year.

It was a lot to text, and Ted was likely to skim over and miss most of it, but at least in text, she had a record of actually saying something to him, where she could point to it and he could understand that it was his fault that he didn't know rather than trying to blame her, as he always did.

She much preferred texting over phone calls because he could totally charm her and lay all the blame at her feet.

It was a while before he texted back, and she was down the beach, her face lifted to the wind, the Gospel of John being spoken in her ear.

That works for me. So we need to figure out
a place to meet on May 24. Here's where I
thought:

Then he sent her a map with a pin drop somewhere in Pennsylvania.

She didn't even look. Knowing him the way she did, he would have found the route, figured the total miles, and pinned the halfway point exactly. There probably wasn't even a rest area there.

She messaged back,

Okay.

She could worry about where the closest exit was when they got to that point. Eventually things would work out, and they would have a place that they normally met, and things would go smoothly.

The thought depressed her. Years from now, she would still be moving her kids back and forth between Boston and Lake Michigan.

She didn't want to think that this was going to go on for so long, but she knew it wasn't going to get better. Not unless one of them died —that would be the only way that they wouldn't be doing this anymore. Because she was never taking him back. Even if he apologized, which he honestly had, but he hadn't meant it. For a while, they'd tried to work it out with him saying that he wouldn't do it again. That was when he'd had the affair with the therapist.

After that, she'd figured that there was no point. Whatever he said was probably not going to be true. And she might as well accept that— the sooner she accepted that, the better off she'd be.

She was still thinking about that while listening to John when she noticed a couple she hadn't seen before walking toward her, holding hands.

As they came closer, it seemed like the woman might be about the same age as she was, in her mid-thirties. The woman didn't have the slender, reed-willow-thin figure of a teenager, and while the man looked athletic and strong, he didn't put her in mind of an older person or a young man either.

She braced herself. They might be people she knew growing up.

Really, she didn't want to see anyone, but there was one person she absolutely did not want to see. Grace.

She had ignored the few messages Grace had left on her phone and completely deleted the number so she wouldn't be tempted to use it at any time.

The area code wasn't from around here, so she'd assumed Grace must've been calling from wherever she'd moved. Chicago? Cleveland? She wasn't sure. Some big city, where Grace had ditched the rest of them, riding out with all the confidence and arrogance of youth. Claire had felt the same way. But she hadn't been quite as flamboyant as Grace had been in her exit.

But Grace was one of the people who knew what had happened, who had gone through the tragedy with her.

And then Claire had deliberately pushed Grace away with her accusations, and they hadn't had a relationship since high school.

And that was really the way Claire wanted to keep it. She had zero desire to revisit the past.

Of course, the Lord was going to put the one person in her path that she didn't want to see.

She knew it was Grace before they were closer than twenty feet. The sea-green eyes, the gorgeous, picture-perfect smile, along with the honey-brown hair that hadn't changed at all.

Grace might have been a little bit heavier than she had been at eighteen, but she definitely wasn't fat. She looked fit and trim and extremely happy to be holding onto the hand of... Could that be Trevor?

Great. Claire now had the perfect reason to not talk to them.

But she couldn't quite manage to make herself continue putting one foot in front of the other when the couple stopped in front of her.

"Good morning. It's a beautiful day for a walk," Grace said, her eyes narrowing, but her voice not holding the familiar recognition that Claire assumed would be there if Grace had recognized her.

"Good morning," Claire said, not adding anything at all to it, hoping that they would just start walking again.

"Claire?" Trevor said. She knew as soon as she heard his voice it was Trevor. She gritted her teeth.

"Yes. It's me. I'm not sure who you two are, but I'd rather keep the past in the past if you don't mind. Have a good day," she said, and then she moved so she could go around them and continued on.

It was rude and unkind, and she could almost feel the two of them turning around and watching her go. But she didn't care. She didn't want to talk to them. Didn't want to dredge up the tragedy, didn't want to have to deal with the past. She had told Josiah that she couldn't have her grandma get sick because she couldn't handle it. She definitely couldn't handle anything popping up from her past. That was all safely buried, and she wanted it to stay that way.

"Claire!"

Claire heard Grace's call, and her first instinct was to continue to walk.

Her feet stopped moving, although she didn't turn around.

"I'd really like to talk to you. Please?"

She wanted to say no. She definitely didn't want to meet with Grace of all people. She sighed and turned partway, but did not look directly at Grace. "Maybe sometime. Not right now, though. I've got to get back, and I need to get my walk in."

She turned around before Grace could suggest that they walk together and started moving quickly.

It was interesting that at that moment, through the speakers, she heard a verse from John about love.

Okay, Lord, I hear You. But can I have a little bit of time to process? To get used to the idea? Do I have to make a spur-of-the-moment decision right this second to meet with her? Surely I'll see her around again. Although maybe Grace was just visiting, and she wouldn't see her around for another year or more.

And she was with Trevor.

She was still stewing about it, although it helped to have the Bible in her ear. She knew she should be kind and was overreacting. She should just be kind. It was that simple. Sometimes simple was hard, though. And this was one of those times, where she knew what she needed to do

—be kind. Just like that. But actually doing it? Totally different story, and not easy at all.

Josiah was already working on the front porch when she walked up to the farmhouse.

Her grandma had said that she was going to sit in the chair and do her devotions, but the last three mornings she'd done that, she'd fallen asleep.

Claire didn't want to go inside and wake her up. Plus, it was a beautiful day—warm and sunny and promised to be the perfect temperature, with a gentle lake breeze keeping the bugs at bay.

She happened to be scraping right along the corner end of the house, almost directly beside where Josiah was working.

She got into the lift, moved it into position, and picked up the torch.

"Have a nice walk?" Josiah said without stopping his work. He was scraping and taking down the railing of the porch. He was going to replace it with a new, more durable type of composite material that would look natural but would last forever, according to the salesperson anyway. Her grandma wanted to try it.

"I guess," she said. And then sighed. She didn't want to talk about this with Josiah, but she wanted to talk about it with someone. And not her grandma either, since she didn't want to upset her grandma. Plus, she knew her grandma would tell her that she needed to be kind. She'd heard that lecture often enough when she was a kid. She doubted it had changed in all the years she'd known her grandma, and she knew her grandma was right.

"That sounded like a 'no' to me," Josiah said, and there was humor in his tone.

"Don't women have the prerogative to say the exact opposite of what they mean?"

"It wasn't quite the exact opposite, but it seems like they take it whether they have it or not," Josiah returned, and there was still humor in his voice. It was like that was something he had accepted from the female gender. She didn't necessarily think it was a good thing, but she knew she had a proclivity toward that. And she didn't consider it lying, even though technically it was. She just considered it...not burdening other people with what she was thinking.

"If you want to talk about it, I'm stuck here for a while, so you can if you want to. I have been told I'm a good listener."

He really was a good listener. Far better than Ted. When she talked to Josiah, he actually heard what she said and remembered it.

He was able to form replies that made sense and have a conversation about it.

Ted had trouble having conversations about anything that didn't directly involve him.

Claire hoped that she was a little better than her husband in that regard, but it seemed like Josiah only got to talk about her life, although he had opened up about his mother the other day.

She should ask about her, but before she did that, she decided she would go ahead and tell him what was bothering her. Maybe it would be too much for him. That would save her from having to talk to him the rest of the day anyway.

"I met Grace on the beach."

"Grace Honea?"

"Yeah. That's probably not her name anymore, but yeah."

"I remember you and she were best friends in high school."

"Until she stole my boyfriend from me."

"He was your boyfriend, was he?" Josiah said immediately, and Claire closed her mouth.

"No. He wasn't." She had to admit that hadn't stopped her from accusing Grace of stealing him. Because Grace knew she liked him. But Trevor had never shown any interest in Claire. He had always had eyes only for Grace, which had made Claire insanely jealous. And even though she wasn't madly in love with Trevor, she had told her friend that she was, just because of the friend code, where friends didn't date a guy that their friend was madly in love with.

Except that had only kept Grace and Trevor apart for a little while. And then they hadn't been able to resist the pull of the two of them together and had gone out together for a while.

Grace had been upset the entire time, though, because Claire wouldn't talk to her.

Claire had used that as an excuse, but in reality, it was just the idea of being around Grace that made the tragedy seem more real. Putting some distance between them made it go away slightly, and she couldn't hardly stand being around Grace, so she'd used the fact that Grace had "stolen" Trevor from her to keep them apart.

It was kind of complicated and really dumb now that she thought about it, but it had seemed to make sense at the time.

"So what was the problem?" Josiah finally prompted when she didn't say anything.

"Remember when Yolanda died?" She hadn't said her name for years, maybe not even for a decade.

"I don't think anybody would forget that."

"I know."

"It was you and Grace out there with her."

"I know."

She didn't want this. She had enough on her plate. But she'd started, so she kept going. "It was hard to be friends with Grace after that. Especially since it didn't feel right without Yolanda with us."

"I always wondered why not. I thought Grace and Lauren felt the same. I'm not sure why. Anyway. Go on."

"So I just said that I liked Trevor. Even when I really didn't."

"I don't understand."

"Yeah. It was...mean, I guess. It was just my little way of torturing Grace. She really liked Trevor. And he was obviously head over heels for her. But they couldn't be together because Grace wouldn't date him because she thought I liked him."

"That gave you a power trip."

"I guess. But it also made it so that Grace couldn't be completely happy. Or something like that. I guess I figured if I was suffering because of the tragedy, she should too."

"And she wasn't?"

"I think she probably was, looking back. She just hid it better than I did. And I didn't understand that even though she didn't look like she was suffering, she was. Maybe I didn't look like I was either."

"But they ended up dating for a while."

"They did. And I was mad at Grace the entire time. I wouldn't talk to her, wouldn't sit with her, talked Lauren into going with me, and generally made her life miserable. I was such a brat."

"Yeah. I'm sorry, but I kind of agree with you. I didn't realize it was that bad."

"Yeah. It was that bad. Eventually, Grace broke up with Trevor because she couldn't stand not being my friend. But it was too late. We had almost graduated, and things were never the same between us. She left in a blaze of glory, determined that she was going to go conquer the world, and I guess I followed not long after, thinking the same thing."

"It's ironic that you're both back here."

"Oh, she's back to stay?" Claire asked, surprised. She'd had in her head that Grace was just visiting.

"Yeah. She moved back early this spring. Maybe late winter. She... moved in with her mom, who appreciated the help, because I'm pretty sure she's getting married."

"My goodness. It's been a long time since I talked to her mom, and she was always so good to us girls." Just the thought alone brought back a ton of memories that she'd thought had been buried forever. They weren't all bad. In fact, most of them were good.

"Yeah. She was a good woman."

"You knew her?" Claire asked, surprised. Not that he knew her necessarily, because it was a small town—of course he knew her. But he wasn't a great friend of Grace's, as far as she knew. She felt an odd sensation inside of her. Uncomfortable and unwelcome. Was that jealousy? Man, she didn't want to be a jealous kind of person.

"I knew her around town. She always had cookies and a smile. I can remember stuff like that. Not that my mom wasn't the same. They were good friends, but after my mom got sick, they didn't lose touch exactly, but Grace's mom lost her husband about the same time, and they just weren't able to get together and comfort each other and everything."

"That's too bad."

It was funny how people lost touch. Sometimes deliberately, like Grace and her, and sometimes not because of any deliberation at all. She hadn't come to see her in a long time, but it wasn't because she didn't love her grandma or want to see her.

"So are you going to get in touch with Grace?" Josiah asked.

"I don't know. I know I should, but I don't really want to."

"You know, you were just telling me earlier that you felt overwhelmed, like if something happened to your grandma, that would be the last thing you could handle. But... You know that Grace could be an ally, right?"

The way he said it made her feel like she was missing an opportunity. And she probably was. He was right. Grace had never been anything but kind to her, even when she hadn't been kind at all. In fact, she'd been deceitful. Maybe that was why she was dragging her feet. If she were to meet with Grace, she'd have to admit what she had done and apologize.

And how selfish is that? When people apologized, it lifted the burden from themselves, not the other person.

But she supposed she'd been raised to think that apologizing was weak. It showed that a person wasn't strong. Which really wasn't true, because it took a lot of courage and guts to apologize. It didn't take anything except stubbornness and nastiness to withhold an apology.

And there she was, being stubborn and nasty.

"Grace was always a really good friend. I don't know why I was so mean to her."

"Grace was perfect," Josiah said offhandedly, like that explained everything.

"You think I was jealous?"

"I didn't say that," he said.

She tried not to get offended, but she felt the irritation rising up in her. Of course he assumed she was jealous of Grace. Who wouldn't be? Grace was gorgeous and, like he said, perfect. She had good grades and everything always went her way.

But wasn't that Claire too? Didn't she get good grades? Other people thought she was fairly good-looking, even if she looked in the mirror and saw all of her flaws. And she had planned on being successful as well. She'd married successfully, according to world standards. Of course, there had been something so terribly wrong with her that her husband wasn't able to stay faithful to her and couldn't work it out even though they'd tried.

That was a little embarrassing, and maybe that was part of the reason she didn't want to talk to Grace. Because she would have to admit what a failure she'd been, where Grace probably had the perfect life.

Although she was with Trevor. So at some point, she'd had issues too. And she was back in Raspberry Ridge.

"Maybe Grace isn't as perfect as what you think she is. She came back for a reason," Josiah pointed out, and it was interesting that Claire's thoughts had been going in that direction already. He just accelerated them.

"You think she's back for the same reasons I am?" she asked, not really hoping. Because she wouldn't hope that kind of pain on anyone. The kind of pain where a person's family exploded, their children were crying, their hopes and dreams were lost in a sea of infidelity and lies and playing around. The kind of pain where a mom had to watch her children go halfway across the country to spend the summer with their dad, knowing that it would be almost three months until she saw them again.

"I don't know. I heard that she and Trevor were back together, though." He stopped scraping for just a moment and leaned back, looking up at her. "It's kind of sad that I know more gossip from around here than you do. You really need to get out more. I'd like to just hand over my man card now."

It was much-needed levity in the conversation, and she laughed.

"I'm sorry. I guess I am depending on you for my gossip. Grandma could probably tell me all this, but... She wasn't feeling the greatest this morning, and I was thinking that she probably was taking a nap after she got done with her devotions."

"Maybe you need to make sure she goes to the doctor," he said casually. Too casually, she thought.

"Really? We talked about this before—you didn't seem to think it was imperative."

"I thought you said you were going to suggest it to her."

"I did. But I was waiting for the right moment. You think I should do it now?"

"I don't think it would hurt," he said, and again, his words sounded studied, like he was weighing them before he said them. It made her suspicious, but she didn't know how to ask what was going on. After all, he wouldn't know anything that she didn't. She was the granddaughter. He was just the hired help.

Grandma wasn't going to talk to him before she'd talk to her.

"Maybe I'll do that when we go in for lunch."

They worked for a few more hours, talking occasionally about light subjects, the weather, ideas for the house, and the kitchen project that he was going to be starting soon. She hated to admit it, but she really did enjoy working and talking with Josiah. He was one of the good guys.

Ten

Josiah felt guilty for not telling Claire about her grandma. He'd dropped as many hints as he possibly could and hoped that if she suggested going to the doctor, her grandma would come out and talk about what she already knew.

Of course, he was sure that Claire was going to be upset with him when she found out that he knew and she didn't. But maybe her grandma wouldn't say. Maybe Claire would figure it out, and maybe he wouldn't be around when it happened.

They quit for lunch around noon. He'd packed a bag lunch, which Claire had stuck in the refrigerator earlier, and she threw a couple of sandwiches together from the leftover homemade bread from the day before.

"No bread today?" he asked as they moved around the kitchen together.

"No. Grandma overslept, and I thought about making it anyway, but I'd rather do it when she's there to help me figure out what I'm doing wrong. My texture just isn't the same as hers, and I'm not sure how to fix it."

"You're doing just fine," Grandma said as she walked into the kitchen.

Josiah thought he'd heard the floorboards creaking, which meant she had gone to her parlor turned bedroom for a nap rather than just napping in her chair. He felt like that was a more serious note than a regular nap.

Claire must've felt that way too, because she didn't hesitate to say what had been on her mind. "Grandma, do you think that maybe it would be a good idea for you to see the doctor? I'm a little bit concerned about you."

Grandma was walking over to the sink, but she paused mid-step, her hand on her cane, her eyes going to her granddaughter before they skittered to Josiah.

Josiah lifted his shoulders and shook his head a little bit.

Then, because he felt a premonition, his eyes moved to Claire, who was looking at him. She'd seen his silent message to Grandma, saying that he hadn't said anything, and she might not have understood exactly what he was saying, but she could tell he'd been hiding something.

Her eyes narrowed, and she didn't have to say anything for him to know that he was in big trouble.

"Let's get some food on the table, and then I need to tell you something," Grandma said.

"All right," Claire said, her voice sounding a little strange. As she set the pitcher of sweet tea on the table, she spoke to Josiah through gritted teeth. "I saw that. You know something."

He lifted his hands in innocence, but what he was really trying to say was he couldn't say anything. Hopefully she would understand and appreciate the fact that he was loyal to her grandma. But he had the feeling she wasn't going to.

They soon had food set on the table, and at some point during the morning, someone had made a salad, and it looked delicious as well.

Josiah said the prayer. Claire didn't waste any time after he was done.

"Grandma? What was it you wanted to tell me?"

Josiah almost interrupted to tell her to let her grandma eat a little bit first, but he kept his mouth shut. He was already in the doghouse.

"Well, I didn't want to worry any family. But a few months ago, I wasn't feeling as perky as I had been, and I started getting these bruises on my arms."

"I knew there was a reason for those bruises," Claire said, narrowing her eyes at her grandma's arms. "Go on," she urged.

"Well, they just did a simple blood test, and it came back that I have leukemia. It's some special kind—I don't remember. But I do remember that the doctor said that he could extend my life with chemotherapy, but most likely he couldn't cure the cancer, and I should consider my quality of life, which would be not as good on the drugs. In fact, he said that if it were his mother, he would suggest that she enjoy the last of her life and not worry about chemo."

"My goodness. Cancer." Claire's hands went to her throat, and her voice wobbled.

Then, smoke seemed to blaze from her ears as her eyes narrowed to slits, and she looked at Josiah.

"You knew." It wasn't a question.

Josiah nodded slowly, watching her the way he would watch a rattlesnake all coiled up and ready to strike at him.

"Don't you get upset with Josiah. He was the one who took me to the doctor's. I wasn't feeling perky enough to drive myself."

"Grandma! I would have taken you!"

"Sweetheart, you had your own problems. Don't you remember how terrible this winter was for you? How broken you were over your husband's infidelity and the breakup of your marriage and the splitting of your family, and how you were trying to sell your house so you could move here, and it was just hard. So many hard things for you. I didn't want to lay any more on you."

"I had the right to know. I should have known. I could have come sooner."

Again, her eyes flew to Josiah. "I can't believe you knew and you didn't tell me."

She shot back away from the table and stormed out of the kitchen and up the stairs. There was a door slam not long after, and Josiah thought that maybe that was kind of like what having teenage daughters would be like.

Maybe it was good that he'd never gotten married.

Although, part of him wanted to go and explain, to beg forgiveness, to somehow make things right between them, because he hated the fact that their relationship had a problem he couldn't solve.

"Should I go talk to her?" he asked Miss Mattie, knowing that he would if she wanted him to although also knowing that there probably wasn't any point in it. Claire was not exactly in the state of mind to be reasoned with.

"Don't you worry about it. When you leave to go back outside, I'll go upstairs and see what I can say to her."

He nodded, knowing that he probably wouldn't see Claire again until Monday. He didn't typically work on the weekends, and he didn't work long days on Monday, Tuesday, and Wednesday when his dad was out of town and he went home for lunch.

He might not see her until next Thursday.

"I'm sorry. I was tempted to tell her, but I thought it was your information to share."

Miss Mattie nodded. "I had asked you not to tell anyone. I wanted to keep it to myself."

"I figured you'd share it if you wanted her to know."

"She's been through so much, I hated to put her through more. I wanted her to get settled here, maybe get reacquainted with some old friends, so she had a bit of a support system around her for when the end happens... Sometimes I think it's not going to be long," Miss Mattie said, looking at the food on the table, and then her eyes dropped down to her plate where she'd only eaten a bite or two.

"Maybe you could eat a bit more?" Josiah suggested. It was the same thing he sometimes said to his mom when she didn't eat. Sometimes he thought that maybe people didn't eat because their bodies were telling them that they just didn't have the energy to digest things, or they needed to put their energy into something else. But whatever it was, he just couldn't see trying to get someone to force-feed themselves.

"I think I've eaten enough. I really didn't have any appetite at all. I came to the table just because I love your company. I'm sorry about my granddaughter."

"No. She's mad at me. And upset about you. She loves you. I think she thought she was going to come back and you guys were going to have a long, long time together."

"She's had a grandmother a lot longer than a lot of people do. Longer than I did. My grandparents all died by the time I was ten. I didn't have anyone growing up."

"That's too bad. I enjoyed spending time with my grandparents, but they're all gone now too."

"It's the way of life. The older generation slowly gives way to the next, and the next, and the next." Somehow, Miss Mattie smiled, and it made things feel like they weren't so bad. He liked being around people who were able to make bad times seem not so bad.

He knew that Claire was going to be upset, but he hoped it was short-lived. And he hoped that she could see that he was doing the best he could under the circumstances.

Because, for some reason, having their relationship not be right bothered him more than he wanted to admit.

Eleven

Claire knew she was acting like a child, but she felt like a child. Her whole world had come crashing down around her in the last year, and now more of it was crashing—more than she even thought she could have crash was crashing.

She knew that bad things happened to people all the time. She didn't expect her life to be trial-free. She didn't expect good things to happen to her on a daily basis and for her never to experience hard times.

But it seemed like this was harder than most, because the hits just kept on coming. *Lord? How much more am I supposed to take?*

She let that question hang in her mind for a bit, but then it seemed like God reminded her that she wasn't supposed to take it alone. She was supposed to give her burdens to the Lord.

But how do I do that? Just dump them on You and walk away?

There was no answer, but in her mind, she thought she heard "yes."

Wasn't that what Jesus said? To cast your burdens on Him because His yoke was easy and His burden light. She was just supposed to give it to God.

And then what? Not worry about Grandma? Pretend Grandma wasn't dying?

That wouldn't be terrible. Grandma would be going to heaven, to be with Jesus. She would be happier.

But life would be sad here without her.

Jesus would still be with her—Claire. Of course there would be sad times. Even Jesus wept when Lazarus died, and that was knowing that He would be raising him from the dead. So it wasn't that people weren't supposed to feel sadness—it was just... They were supposed to trust the Lord and keep walking on.

Precious in the sight of the Lord is the death of His saints.

She wasn't sure why that verse popped into her mind. After all, Grandma wasn't dead yet. But she was dying. Of that there was no doubt.

"Claire?" She heard a soft rap on her door, and then her grandma's voice again. "Claire?"

"Come on in, Grandma," she said, straightening herself off the bed and wiping the tears off her face. She was angry at Josiah because he knew. He knew, and he hadn't told her. That made her so mad she wanted to grab a hold of his neck and just shake it. And she wasn't usually prone to violence.

"Oh, sweetheart," her grandma said, out of breath from climbing the stairs and tottering a bit even with her cane.

"I'm sorry you had to climb the stairs. You really didn't have to come up. I was going to come down as soon as Josiah left."

"He's gone, but... I did want to talk to you about that."

"Grandma. He didn't tell me that you were sick! You didn't tell me. Don't you know that I would want to know that?"

"And don't you know that you were already going through so much? I wanted to protect you. You are my granddaughter. I love you."

"I love you too. And I want to know when there's something wrong." She paused, then tilted her head. "Don't you want to know when there's something wrong with me?"

Grandma's gnarled hand slid across the bedspread—one she had made with her own fingers, those same fingers, more than two decades ago. Claire remembered Grandma sitting in her chair that summer, quilting as her grandchildren played around her, coming and going. She was a teenager at the time, and she'd stopped, eaten cookies and drunk tea and talked to her grandma, and then run off again with her friends.

She couldn't quite remember, but that was probably a couple of summers after she'd kissed Josiah.

"Of course I do. I didn't want... I was going to tell you. I didn't really want to keep it away from you, but I wanted you to get settled some, get a support system around you. Have you made any friends yet since you've come back?"

"I talked to Grace this morning."

"There. Grace will be good for you. See? If I'd told you earlier, you wouldn't know Grace was back."

She didn't want to argue with her grandma, so she just kept her mouth closed. "Josiah should have told me. I went to him about your bruises, I talked to him. He pretended he didn't know anything."

Grandma was quiet for a moment, just softly stroking Claire's hand, and then she said, "I think that one of the best things a Christian can do is determine that no matter what someone does to them, they are not going to get offended over it. They're just going to let all the hard things slide off their backs."

"What person can do that?" Claire said without even thinking about it.

"Well, with the spirit of the Lord, we can. Because after all, Christ Himself commanded us to be kind to those who persecute us. We are commanded to not just not get offended—we're supposed to be kind. And I think you'll find if you practice that, your life gets a lot easier and less stressful if you're not constantly being upset over what someone else might have done, might've said, or might have that you want. Just determine that you're not going to get upset."

She stared at her grandma. The idea was novel. Not get upset? But immediately she could see the advantages. After all, she'd just been miserable for how long? And before that, for almost an entire year she'd been offended and upset over what her husband had done. What if she just hadn't gotten upset? What if she had just given it to God, which she'd been thinking about before, and not worried about it? The idea was not completely novel, but it was utterly intriguing. Because she wanted to live a life of calmness and peace, the way her grandmother seemed to have.

"Is that your secret?"

Grandma smiled. "It might be one of them. But I don't think it's a secret. If it is, I'm sharing it with you now."

Claire smiled. "You know I'm not going to be able to do this overnight, right?"

"Of course not. I didn't do it overnight either. It was a lifetime of deciding that no matter what people did to me, I wasn't going to get upset with them. I was unsuccessful most of the time at first, but the more I determined that I wanted to be like Jesus—kind, compassionate, levelheaded even when the Pharisees were constantly trying to trip Him up—the better I got at it. And the happier my life was. It's funny how happy you are when you're not busy getting upset with people."

"So I can get upset with situations?" Claire was mostly teasing, because she was pretty sure her grandma was talking about people and situations.

"Your life will be a lot happier, a lot easier, a lot less stressful, if you just give it to God. Just admit that it's in God's hands, and He's going to do what He wants to, and it's going to be the best for you."

"I just can't see how losing you could be best for me. Or best for my children. We'll miss you."

"I'll live on. You'll make sure that I do. In fact, you might remember the things that I said even better when I'm not around to state them anymore." Her grandma chuckled a little and continued to stroke her hand.

Claire couldn't find that funny, even though she wanted to laugh.

"Now, I'm not telling you what you need to do with Josiah, but you know he was between a rock and a hard place. He knew that if I'd wanted you to know, I would have told you. He also knew that you would want to know. So he had to make a choice. And he chose to honor the trust that I had placed in him when I'd asked him to take me to the doctor's."

She still felt corrosive anger when she thought about Josiah knowing and not telling her. There was mostly the fact that she felt she deserved to know. Maybe that was pride. Maybe it was pride making her feel like someone should have told her. Who was she to expect anyone to let her know anything?

"Maybe humility is the key to not being offended?" she said, knowing that her grandma was probably the most humble person she knew. After all, she never insisted that she deserved anything. She just put her hand in Jesus's hand and walked softly along beside Him. And whatever came, she handled it with Jesus by her side.

"I think you might be on the right track with that."

"Well, maybe I ought to go outside and apologize to Josiah while I'm still thinking I can. I've found that the longer I let things go, the harder it is to apologize."

She thought again about Grace. She really needed to apologize to her, but decades had gone by, and how was she going to start? She didn't want to dredge up old things that had been covered over and buried. Sometimes they hurt worse the second time around. But sometimes they just lay there and festered. For her, it was fine—she didn't care if she ever talked about it again. But maybe Grace would need to hear her apologize. Plus, she probably would feel a little bit lighter and less guilty and wouldn't keep thinking about it if she managed to apologize and get it off her chest.

"I think it would be a good idea. That boy thinks a lot of you, and I could tell it was really upsetting him that there was something between you."

"I didn't have any right to get upset. I shouldn't have. I mean, I would have liked it if you would have told me, but you're right. He was doing you a favor, and who am I to deserve to have that information anyway?"

Grandma smiled at her, and then she grimaced a little as she shifted. "I think I'm going to go find a pain pill and maybe take a nap."

"Grandma?"

"Yes?" Her grandma paused as she shifted to get off the bed.

"Have the doctors given you anything for pain?"

"Not yet. I haven't been in any kind of pain to need anything. But... Maybe it's time to make another visit. They said eventually they would need to give me stronger and stronger pain meds, and then perhaps morphine. They said that with morphine, the end would not be hard.

I... The one thing I asked when I went was that death be painless. As painless as it can be.”

Claire swallowed. She didn’t want to talk about death. Especially her grandma’s death, but she had to be brave, because Grandma was trusting her with this information. “I can make an appointment if you tell me where the number to your doctor is.”

“I’ll find it when I get downstairs. And the other thing I asked was that I be able to die at home. They said that shouldn’t be a problem. They talked about hospice. Do you have any experience with that?”

“No experience, but I’ve heard of them. I guess the doctor will tell us when it’s time to call them.”

She was surprised she’d found the bravery to say those words. She didn’t want to. She wanted to go bury herself somewhere, where she didn’t have to deal with this. She needed some time to process. Some time to think. And... Maybe a shoulder to cry on.

Josiah came to mind, but then she thought about Grace.

It wasn’t a coincidence that she had met Grace just that morning. God orchestrated everything, and there was no doubt in her mind that God had brought Grace into her life just when she would need her the most. Except she should have responded to Grace when she had left messages on her phone, reaching out. Perhaps now Grace would be upset with her and not open to reconciliation. But if that were the case, it was her own fault. And she had no one but herself to blame.

“I can help you,” she said as Grandma grimaced again.

“Some days, it’s not bad. I think it was the rain that we had earlier, or maybe the rain that’s coming.”

Claire didn’t say anything. She highly doubted it had anything to do with the rain, but there was no point in arguing with Grandma. It might’ve been her grandma’s way of thinking that things would get better. And she supposed that was a positive and healthy way to look at things. It would at least keep Grandma’s spirits up, and Claire wasn’t going to do anything to dash her hopes. Maybe, maybe when they went to the doctor, he would be able to tell her that there was still hope that Grandma would pull through. That she would have lots of pain-free and happy years ahead. She hoped so.

Twelve

Josiah was in the act of trying to pry the porch railing back away from the post when Claire came out the door.

He realized he was holding his breath but couldn't seem to make his lungs work as her eyes met his.

Her face seemed calmer, and maybe she wasn't angry anymore. Was it possible that she'd gotten over it that fast?

His dad had always said that his mom was not really a normal woman because she never got angry. His dad told horror stories of growing up with sisters who fought over everything and got offended over the slightest things.

Maybe Josiah was using an unfair yardstick with which to measure Claire.

"I'm sorry. I stomped away angry, and that was really immature and stupid of me."

"It's okay. I kind of figured when we were talking that you were going to be angry when you found out. But... I couldn't say anything, because I knew that if your grandma wanted you to know, she would have told you. As much as I wanted you to know." He wanted her to believe that. Because it was true. He had almost told her over and over again, because he thought it was important for her to know.

"That makes me feel a little better. I'm glad that you wanted me to know, at least."

"Is she okay?" he asked, referring to her grandma.

She nodded. "She admitted everything and agreed that maybe she needed to go back to the doctor. She's in pain now."

She closed her eyes and put a hand out to steady herself against the doorpost.

He set his tools down, straightened, and walked up the steps.

"Want to sit down for a minute?" he said, afraid she was going to fall down if she didn't find a place to rest for a moment.

"I just can't believe it. My grandma. I mean... I wanted her to be my rock. And now I come here, and she's just another problem." She put her head in her hands. "I don't mean it like that." She sighed, rubbing her fingers over her forehead, as though she had a headache. "I just mean it like... I wanted to come here and heal, not have more to deal with."

"Apparently the Lord had other plans," he said, knowing that she was just as liable to get upset with him for saying it as she was to be comforted by it.

She looked up. "Grandma said that I should be careful not to be offended. She said that my life will be a lot less stressful if I learn to just let things go. Not just the things people do, but situations too. Like Grandma." She lifted a hand and held it out. "I can't do anything about it. Worrying isn't going to solve anything. So I just need to trust God. But you know how much harder it is to do that than it is to say?"

He grinned a little. "Yeah, I've had decades of experience with my mom."

Realization dawned in her eyes, and her head tilted a bit. "I'm sorry. I'm making my problem huge, while you have your own problems."

"But I've dealt with them. I've done what you just said. What your grandma told you to do. God's got it. And yeah, sometimes I look at her and think, 'Man, I think she's worse than she used to be,' or 'Is that another symptom? Does that mean she's going downhill faster?' But then I remember that it's not up to me to know the times or the seasons. I just have to trust that God's going to keep her here with me until it's time for her to go. And of course, I'm going to do everything I can to make her more comfortable, to follow the doctor's orders, to help her eat healthy and hopefully extend her life. But in the end, God is in control, and I have to pry my fingers off and let it go."

He'd never really said it that clearly to anyone before, but it seemed like Claire could use a little help. She seemed overwhelmed.

"Thank you for that. I guess that's what I need to do. But it's so hard to think of the future without her."

"Why do you need to think about that now?" he asked. He'd long ago stopped wondering what things would be like when his mom passed. After all, he could sit around worrying about that for years and end up dying first. It was a silly thing to worry about.

"I guess I don't," she said after a moment of thought. "I just feel like I have to figure everything out this second."

"Isn't that what faith is? Just knowing that God will figure it out. We don't have to. When the time comes, God's going to give us grace to get through whatever it is we need to get through, and if we need to figure something out, we'll figure it out then."

"That's such a more relaxed way of looking at it. I want to worry. I feel like I *need* to worry. If I'm not worrying, then I'm not doing my job."

"The Bible says that worry is sin," he said, not meaning to argue with her, but he knew he was right. And he knew that she would understand when she heard it, because she'd been talking about it.

"I know. Why do I feel like I need to, when the Bible clearly tells me I don't?"

"Maybe that's Satan trying to convince us that what God said isn't relevant. He does it all the time, you know."

He thought about how people felt like it was important that they not be doormats, and if someone wasn't kind to them, they were being a doormat if they were kind in return. So many things the Bible clearly said were not God's will, and yet Christians quickly did what the world said and hardly ever tried to put the Bible into practice in their life. They read it, and the words went right over their head.

"I think it just feels better to me to be doing what isn't right sometimes. And that surprises me, because I thought I was very sensitive to sin."

"Sure. You probably are. Sins like lying and cheating and being unkind. But sins like worry and fear and treating other people the way they treat us aren't really on our radar all the time."

"Or pride. I finally figured out that part of the reason I was offended that you didn't tell me that my grandma was sick was because I thought I deserved to know. That's pride. I...have a problem with that. Feeling like I deserve things."

"I guess we don't deserve anything but hell. But it's hard to reconcile that."

"It is. It is hard to take that a step further and be grateful for every little thing we get, because that isn't what we deserve."

"Sometimes we get something, and we feel like we need even more on top of that, rather than being grateful for what we get."

"Guilty," she said, smiling at him.

He wanted to ask if she was feeling better. She looked like it. Finally, she took a deep breath and then looked out over the horizon.

"Thank you. I feel better. Maybe not able to handle everything, but at least armed with the knowledge that there's nothing I can do, and I might as well let go and give God the control that I want to desperately wrestle away from Him. And why?" She laughed. "Because I think I can do so much better? There's pride again. I don't think God is handling it well enough, so I need to grab it from Him and take control."

"We all do that, right?"

"Thanks for talking to me." She looked over at him and looked grateful. It made his heart swell a bit, and he just nodded, then looked away. He didn't want to have any tender moments between them, because he knew that she was just seeing him as a friend. And he also knew that there was a part of him that could want more. And shouldn't.

"I think I'm going to do what you suggested and reach out to Grace. I think it was pride keeping me from it. After all, who wants to apologize? And that's the first thing I need to do."

"You might be surprised. She might not remember things the way you do, and she probably isn't expecting an apology."

"Are you defending her?" Claire asked, causing his eyes to slant to hers.

She had been joking.

"I might have been a little bit."

"You're not allowed to do that. Not until we're friends again. And then, once Grace and I are friends, then you can defend her all you want to."

"I'll keep that in mind," he said. "You keep me posted."

"I will." They sat there for a moment, and then she said, "Thanks again. I appreciate your listening ear and your wisdom. I needed it to kind of get out of my slump. Whatever happens, happens, and I'm going to trust God and hold onto Him." She put a hand up. "Which does not mean that I'm not going to miss my grandma. But she's not gone yet, so I don't have to think about that now."

"That's right. Something will come, something better, and God will work it all out for good."

She smiled at him one last time before she got up and walked around the edge of the house.

He sat there for another moment, thinking. He had briefly mentioned fear as being a sin. And maybe that's what had kept him from dating all of these years—because he knew how Claire hadn't responded to his kiss all those years ago, when he had enjoyed it. Maybe that had marked him, caused him to be afraid, more than he realized.

But maybe too, he was waiting for someone more like Claire to come along. Now Claire herself was here, and he was afraid to have any deep moments with her, because he was afraid she wouldn't feel the way he did. Fear. He didn't want to allow fear to control his life, and yet...he was. Maybe that was something he needed to work on.

Thirteen

It was the weekend with her kids home, and Claire wanted to enjoy the time that she had left with them. Then, on Monday her grandma had an appointment with her doctor, and Josiah was gone, working on a yacht.

She missed him more than she thought. She hadn't seen him since they'd sat on the porch and talked and she'd apologized—it hadn't even been a week, but she found she missed his steady presence.

But she also realized that she'd been grasping at people to fill the spot where God was supposed to be. She wanted someone she could depend on. Someone who would steadily and unfailingly help her through these hard times. Wasn't that the position of God Himself? And yet, she'd wanted her grandma to do that, and then she was counting on Josiah thinking how he could do it for her and wanting to reach out to Grace so that she would have someone.

They were sitting in the waiting room waiting for the doctor to call them back when she finally realized that it was okay to depend on people. It was okay to allow people to comfort her, to help her, to encourage her the way Josiah had. After all, God had given her people to surround herself with, to help her. Christians were supposed to band together and walk through this difficult life.

She just had to be careful that she wasn't putting people in the position that God was supposed to be in—leading her and guiding her and being the one she could depend on always.

Because people were going to let her down. Either they were going to die like Grandma, cheat like her husband, or make mistakes, maybe like Grace, although those mistakes seemed like they were more hers.

They wouldn't be perfect, like Josiah.

Although the more time she spent with him, the more she felt like maybe he had grown into someone who was...more perfect than he used to be, anyway. But he didn't seem interested in her like that at all anymore. He'd laughed about their kiss and didn't seem the slightest bit offended when she'd said that it hadn't been what she had hoped it would be—that she had been disappointed in it.

She probably shouldn't have said that. She knew that male egos were fragile, and if she would have said that to her ex-husband, he would have gotten angry and attacked her back.

"Mrs. Donegan, come on back. We'll get your weight and vitals, and then the doctor will be in to see you."

Grandma stood, obviously in pain. It hurt Claire's heart to see it. And she wished that there was something she could do.

She reminded herself, she was doing something.

"Claire's coming with me," Grandma said as she moved slowly back toward the hall where the nurse led them.

Claire hated the idea that Grandma had done this by herself lots of times before. But she had to remind herself that she'd always felt better. This was the worst that she'd felt, and Claire was grateful that the Lord had allowed her to be here.

She braced herself, because she was afraid to hear what the doctor was going to have to say. But at least the doctor was compassionate, concerned, and sympathetic.

"We can start hospice anytime. They'll take over managing her care, regulating her meds, and keeping her comfortable—that will be their main goal." The doctor looked down at her iPad. "In the meantime, I can prescribe some stronger pain meds. These will take the pain away, but they'll knock her out as well. It's a matter of giving up one for the other."

Her grandma nodded, understanding. She would be sleeping more and interacting less, but the pain would be gone.

"Is there something I could take during the day to just dull it a little?" her grandma asked.

"You can take over-the-counter pain meds, and I can give you increased dosages that would be safe for you to take." The doctor paused. "These would not be normal dosages that normal people could take, but since we're looking at end-of-life care, we're not worried about kidney function or liver enzymes—we're just worried about comfort at this point. Do you understand?"

Grandma nodded.

Claire managed not to start crying, but she had to bite down hard on her cheeks to keep her eyes from filling with tears. This was the beginning of the end. But it didn't really help anything to think that way. And she reminded herself that birth was actually the beginning of the end. Maybe conception. Everything was decaying even as it was growing. And there was always an end. It was always there. They were just getting closer.

"If you want to see any family, if you want to have any get-togethers, if anyone wants to talk to you for the last time, I would highly recommend you make that happen in the next few weeks." At this point, her eyes lifted to Claire's, who nodded. "I don't want to scare you, because I think we can keep the pain managed. I don't think there will be any fear, any pain—it's going to be a smooth transition. But your hours of being able to be awake and talking to people and thinking about your last will and that type of thing are going to be limited. So you're going to want to get those things done if you can."

She appreciated the doctor being straightforward with them and not trying to give them false hope. Death was not an easy thing to think about, and it was even harder to talk about, but these were the conversations that she needed to have.

"How much longer does she have?" Claire finally managed to ask, and her voice was calm and steady.

The doctor smiled sadly. "I wish I could give you an exact time. I know that's what you want. But all I can say is... I don't know. Honestly. She could pass away in her sleep tonight. It's unlikely," the doctor said quickly, when she saw Claire's eyes widen, "but it's possible. Or she could make it to Christmas. If she does, I would plan on having a really big celebration, because it will probably be her last. I would say no more than six months." Her voice lowered, and it was full of sympathy and sadness as she delivered the last timeframe.

Less than six months. Next spring, she would welcome the warmer air and the flowers and the roses blooming without her grandma. She'd make bread this winter without her. She'd get her children back from her husband, and it was possible Grandma wouldn't be there.

She wanted to sob. She wanted to put her head down and cry, but she couldn't. She had to suck up all the tears she wanted to just allow to flow and put a hand on her grandmother's hand.

Her grandma turned her hand, and their fingers clasped together. Grandma's hand was old, her skin soft and loose. But so familiar. So beloved.

"I'll be seeing Jesus in less than a year. That's the good news. Thanks for giving it to me straight," her grandmother said to the doctor.

The doctor looked a little surprised and then shrugged a bit, as though everyone had their own way of facing it, and she wasn't going to tell Grandma any different. "You can call me anytime. My office will fulfill any of the prescription needs. If the pain meds run low, if you need help sleeping, just let us know. We can be very free with whatever will keep her comfortable. Also, hospice will be the same. I promise. They're in the business of keeping people comfortable and at home while they pass from this world to the next."

With that, the doctor asked if they had any more questions, and then she exited the room.

Grandma had gotten dressed, but it took a little while for her to get out of the chair.

They needed to stop at the nurses' station to pick up their scripts, and once they did that, they stepped out of the building into the beautiful, blinding sunshine.

"Such a pretty day." Her grandma looked around. "Would it upset you if I said it's a beautiful day to learn that you're going to go be with Jesus?"

"No. I don't think so. It's a really good way to look at it. I'm a little jealous."

"I get to see my parents again. And see my husband. I lost a son, and he'll be there too. I... I'm almost happy. Except..." She turned her head and looked at Claire. "You look sad. It breaks my heart that you're so sad. Be happy for me. This is a happy day." Grandma lowered her head, trying to look into Claire's eyes.

They had filled with tears, and to her dismay, one of them spilled over.

"I'm trying. I'm trying really hard to think of you and not me. When I think of me, all I can do—all I want to do—is cry."

"I wanted to have the kitchen done before I left. I wanted to leave you with a house that had all the repairs done on it. I...put you in my will to get the house. Everything else has to be split up with everyone else. But the house is yours. The farm. Take good care of it."

"I don't want anything!" Claire cried out. "I just want you!" She knew she was being unreasonable. Grandma was the one who was being thoughtful and considerate, making sure that there wouldn't be any fights after her death, making sure that Claire was taken care of, being happy for the situation that she couldn't change, accepting it, and focusing on the good. And all Claire could do was think about how much this was going to hurt and how much she didn't want to lose her grandma.

But they were in a public parking lot, and she needed to pull herself together. If not for the people watching, then for Grandma. Because her grandma had just said that the one thing that was making her sad was the fact that Claire was sad.

She vowed in her heart that she would try to be happy for Grandma's sake.

Lord, she's going home. And that's a good thing. Help me to focus on that.

"All right, Grandma. It's a happy day. Look at the sunshine. See the tulips blooming. It's a beautiful day to learn you're going to meet Jesus."

Her grandma smiled, nodded, and then took Claire's arm with her free hand, using her cane with the other, as they slowly made their way to the car so they could go home and she could take a nap.

Fourteen

Josiah sat on the bench at the waterfall in the healing garden at Raspberry Ridge. He'd worked the weekend and finished the job on the yacht, which hadn't taken very long—only a couple of days—and he'd gotten ready to go to work this morning at Miss Mattie's house, knowing Miss Mattie and Claire wouldn't be there, since Miss Mattie had a doctor's appointment.

He'd come home for lunch with his mother and had gotten the text from Miss Mattie, letting him know that they were going to be calling hospice.

Rather than going back to work, he'd gone to the healing garden to sit and think. Claire was going to be devastated. And he didn't know if he had the words to help her. Or whether he even should try. What did he know about death and dying? Other than the fact that he knew that his mom had an autoimmune disease that was never going to be healed, and he'd resigned himself to that and the fact that she could die at any moment years ago.

And yet she had hung on. And there was Claire, who had just recently—in the last week—found out that Grandma was dying of cancer, and now she needed to deal with hospice and all the things that entailed.

He wanted to send her a text. Ask her if she needed him to do anything. Ask if they wanted him to start the big kitchen project, which is what he was getting ready to do, now that they knew there would be a funeral in the near future.

Of course, he didn't know how near the future was. And he wanted to ask that, but that didn't exactly seem like the kind of question one shot off in a text to someone that one wasn't even sure was one's friend, let alone someone that he could talk to about stuff like that.

"Josiah." A man's voice interrupted his thoughts. He was surprised, because often people just nodded or waved at the healing garden and didn't actually talk to anyone.

He looked around to see Trevor. He'd talked to Trevor some at church and knew him from growing up. They weren't best friends, even though they both lived in Raspberry Ridge and had chosen to stay to take care of their parents. Trevor had just moved back not that long ago, and Josiah figured that he probably could really enjoy being around each other if they had the time.

But Trevor had developed a relationship with Grace, and his dad had developed a relationship with Grace's mom, and between the busyness of Trevor's life and all the things going on with Josiah, they just hadn't had a whole lot of time.

"Hey, Trevor," he said, standing up from the bench.

Trevor put a hand out. "I didn't mean to interrupt you."

"You're not. I came home to eat with my mom, and I had a little bit of extra time before I needed to get back to work at Miss Mattie's house. But it's time for me to leave now."

"Well, I don't want to keep you. But... I was looking for a chance to talk to you."

"All right," he said. "I've got time. I keep my own hours, so I can show up when I want to." He didn't add that Miss Mattie had a doctor's appointment that morning.

That wasn't really his news to share, although Miss Mattie hadn't told him not to tell anyone.

"I know that you spend a lot of time at Miss Mattie's house, and I didn't know if you and Claire have been talking, but Grace asked me to say something to you if I ran into you anywhere."

"I've spoken with Claire some. And... I think she wants to talk to Grace. I think sometimes those things need—a person just needs a little bit of time to get up the nerve, you know?"

"Did she say that Grace was mad?" Trevor asked, sounding surprised.

"I think she just feels like she needs to give an apology, and sometimes that can feel like an insurmountable thing. After all, if apologies were easy, it wouldn't be such a big deal."

"True." Trevor nodded. "But I guess you kind of answered her question. Grace wanted to know if Claire was still mad at her, because she's reached out to Claire several times and Claire hasn't responded."

"Claire's been going through a good bit. I'm guessing that she probably felt like she couldn't handle even one more thing, but that's just me guessing."

"All right. Good to know. If she's not actively upset, Grace thought she might try reaching out again."

"I really think Claire could use a friend. I'm not even sure that she knows how much she could use one."

Trevor's face became thoughtful, but he just nodded. "There are always times in our lives when we need friends. And I've never found that having too many friends was a bad thing."

"Sometimes it's hard for me to keep up with everybody. I want to be a good friend, but that takes so much time and work that I feel like I can only have one or two."

Maybe he was just being weird. Maybe it was a man thing. But he wanted to be a good friend, and he couldn't do that with a whole pile of people.

"Yeah, I guess you could have a few and go deep, or you can have a lot and just be surface friends. Different personalities prefer different ways."

Josiah nodded. "Congratulations to you and Grace. I heard that there is a marriage in your future soon."

"Thanks." Trevor's face lit up. "There is. And our parents got married. Did you hear that?"

"I did. Congratulations again, I guess. Lots of marriages going around."

And a death. But he didn't say that. Again, it really wasn't his news.

"Maybe you'll have one in your future."

"I think we're the only two bachelors in our class. And... If I got married, I wouldn't be representing the bachelors very well, would I?"

He was making light of the situation. It wasn't that he didn't want to get married. He would like to. But he had the feeling that women looked at a man in his thirties who wasn't married and who still lived with his parents and figured that there was probably something wrong with him. Some reason why other women hadn't been willing to give him a chance.

"Maybe I'm too old," he muttered, not really expecting Trevor to say anything.

"Don't forget, we're the same age, and I'm engaged for the first time."

"Good point. I didn't mean to insinuate that you were too old."

"I always thought Claire had a thing for you. I know that she always acted like she had something for me, but we both know she didn't. And there was that truth or dare game."

Josiah grinned. Was the whole class there that day? "It's funny. The only person I remember being there that day was Claire. And...yeah. Maybe she didn't have a thing for me, but I had a thing for her. And I wonder how long that lasted."

"You dated around. I saw you with some other girls."

"I did." None of them were Claire. None of them took. Maybe it wouldn't have mattered that they weren't Claire, if they had been exceptionally interested in him. But he hadn't found anyone like that.

"All right. I'll quit bugging you about it. I guess when a guy gets happy, he wants everyone to be as happy as he is. It's funny, because I've never been a matchmaker."

"And yet you got your parents together."

"Did you hear about that?"

Josiah laughed. "It's a small town, remember?"

"All right. I'll just leave it at that. Grace will be in touch with Claire. She'll be happy to know that Claire is not angry. I hope they can work it out. Grace really wants to put the past behind her and rekindle her old friendship with Claire."

"I hope they can too. I think it will be good for everyone involved."

The tragedy loomed large over the whole town, and if the friends could get back together and put it behind them, he couldn't imagine that everyone wouldn't benefit. Including him.

Fifteen

"How did it go?"

Josiah stood on the lift, scraping paint. He'd already talked to Claire, who had asked him to give her a hand with painting the house after she'd found out about her grandma.

He'd seen them come home a little earlier from their doctor's appointment and had been dying of curiosity, but had not stopped working. His conversation with Trevor had been at the top of his mind too, and he wanted to talk to Claire about Grace. But he already knew she had heaps of things on her plate. The last day of school was sometime soon. That would have her stressed out as well.

"I don't know. Good, I guess," she said, coming around the corner with two glasses of tea in her hand. "Do you want to take a break?" she asked, holding a glass of tea out.

"Sure," he said. He wasn't going to turn down tea, but more than that, he wasn't going to turn down time with her. If she wanted to talk, he was going to be there for her. Even if they never became anything more, he knew enough to know that that was what friends were for.

He lowered the lift so that it sat on the ground and then opened the gate and stepped off. "Thanks. Go sit down. You look like you're about ready to fall."

"I'm just tired. It was…emotional."

"Okay," he said as they went and sat down on the small bench in the yard. He had the porch mostly torn apart, propped up by two-by-fours, with the porch swing down and the rocking chairs in the shed.

"Thanks for the tea," he said as they sat and he took a sip, waiting for her to start talking. He didn't know what question to ask. She'd said it went well. But she looked exhausted and not especially happy.

"The doctor said six months."

"That's not terrible. You have plenty of time to say goodbye—"

"No. Well, I guess to be more specific, she said she could die in her sleep tonight, but the longest that she would give her would be six months. She said if we were able to spend Christmas together, she would make a big deal of it because it would be her last for sure."

"That's not very encouraging."

"No. The doctor was very sympathetic. I felt bad that she had to give such terrible news. I wouldn't want to have a job where I had to tell people that they were dying in the next six months."

"Yeah, me neither," he said, grateful that he was just a handyman and fix-it person. He couldn't imagine if his job included playing God, even in that small way.

"Anyway. I'm supposed to call all the relatives and let them know. She said that we could give Grandma as much pain medicine as she wanted, but the more and stronger the pain medicine got, the more Grandma would sleep and be out of it." She took a breath, looking at her tea but not touching it. "Grandma said she'd like to try to hold off on the pain meds until everyone who wanted to see her had been around to talk. I'm glad she's lucid enough to think that way."

"Me too."

"But I just feel so overwhelmed. I need to make all the phone calls, the last day of school is tomorrow, and my kids have a program that night, and I don't know whether to try to take Grandma or have her stay, and whether to stay with her and—"

He put a hand up. "Hey. I'll help. Okay? If you need to stay with Grandma, I can take the kids. And if you want to go with the kids, I can stay with Grandma. You make the decision and tell me what you need." He said that as firmly but as calmly as possible. He didn't want to put any pressure on her, but he wanted her to know that she was not alone. He also wanted to say that it was too bad she hadn't been able to get in touch with Grace, because he was sure that Grace would help her through this hard time.

But it was probably too late to try to form any type of bond, especially now while Claire was in such panic mode.

Still, if the opportunity came up, he might mention his conversation with Trevor.

"Thank you so much. I... I guess I just feel overwhelmed. But I appreciate you being calm and reasonable."

"I think it's easier for me, because it's not my life that's imploding."

"But you're sympathetic enough to make me feel like you care while still keeping me grounded."

"I'm glad it's working. I want to help you any way I can."

"I'm going to have to figure out how to get the kids to my husband —ex-husband—as well."

"I'll help you with that."

"Thanks." She gave him a reassuring smile. "Grandma and I decided that we were going to try to do as many things together this last week as we could. I... I don't expect the kids will get to see her again alive. And I haven't decided whether I should try to get them back for the funeral."

"You might want to talk to them about it. They might not want to come back. Or they might feel like they need to."

"Do you think they're old enough to make that decision?"

"I think if you talk to them about it and tell them that you'd like to do the thing that works best for them—the thing they want, even if it isn't what they think they should want—they'll remember that you at least talked to them about it."

"Good point. I guess what is the right decision for one kid could be a wrong decision for another, and who am I to know whether it's best or not?" She seemed to be thoughtful as she said that. He was glad that she seemed to be able to reason things out and didn't seem to be in quite such a panic. "All right. I still feel like everything's a jumble in my brain."

"You need to make some phone calls, you need to be here when your kids get off the bus, you have a program tomorrow night, and you can let me know if you want me to go see the kids or if you want me to stay with Grandma. Or maybe she feels well enough that between the two of us we can get her there."

"Oh, that would be best. Yeah. Let's aim for that, if you don't mind helping."

"No. I don't. My dad's not here right now, so I just might not work as many long hours here, go home and spend some time with my mom, and then come back and spend the evening with you. She's often in bed shortly after supper anyway."

"Oh, I hate to take you away from her."

"Don't worry about it. I told you, I'll see her during the day. I don't have any yacht work this week either, and I might cancel next week's job."

"I don't want you to lose any work."

"I'm not losing work. I'll just postpone it until some other time. Things come up. And if they find someone else to do the job, it's not like I need it. I promise. I won't do anything that jeopardizes my financial health."

"Well, thank you. I'll trust that you'll keep your word on that and tell me if I'm asking too much of you."

"I'll let you know." He paused, draining the last of his tea before he said casually, "I talked to Trevor today."

"You did?"

He nodded. "I was at the healing garden in town. You know where I mean?"

"I've been there once since I moved here. I wanted to explore it a little more. Grandma talks so well about it, but I just haven't made the time."

"You should. Vera and her husband did a great job on it. Anyway, I had lunch with my mom, and then I went there for a few minutes. Trevor found me there, and we chatted."

"Is he engaged to Grace?" Claire asked, seeming to forget all of her other problems in her interest in Trevor and Grace.

"I think so. He said there was going to be a wedding soon. And that his dad and her mom just got married."

"So you were right."

He nodded. "My mom has her ways, and I get everything from her."

"I just found out your secret, right?"

"Sure did." He grinned at her and was gratified to see her smiling. If teasing him made her happy, she could go at it all she wanted to. "He asked about you. He wanted to know if you were angry. He said Grace was afraid that you were because she'd tried to reach out to you and you hadn't responded."

"He's right. She's reached out several times, and I just haven't."

"I explained that you have a lot on your plate right now. That you were going through a good bit. I didn't get into a bunch of details, because I didn't know how much you wanted to share with everyone."

"I might as well share everything there is, because being that it's a small town, everyone's going to figure it all out anyway."

"I don't know. If Trevor knew more than what I told him, he didn't let on. But that's your call. Just know that Grace really wants to get together, and I know she'd be a help right now."

She nodded and didn't seem too upset about the suggestion. He was afraid she was going to get defensive, but he couldn't go around being scared that she would get upset every time he opened his mouth.

And she really wasn't that kind of person anyway.

He wasn't sure why he was so cautious, unless it was all the stories his dad had told about irrational women. He was starting to think that maybe the stories weren't true.

Or maybe, just maybe, he'd found a gem in Claire.

But only as a friend. She certainly hadn't indicated that she wanted anything more.

"All right. I still think I'm a little fuzzy in my head about everything I need to do, but kids first, tomorrow. Maybe I can... Did he leave Grace's number?"

"No. I didn't think to ask for it. But my mom might have it, or I can get her number. You want me to text it to you later?"

"Yes. If you're able to get it, please pass it along to me. I shouldn't have deleted everything from my phone. But I was certain at the time that there would never be a time when I would want to...get back together with her."

"Friends can be invaluable, and I have a feeling that you're going to need a pretty strong support system. You know you can depend on people in the town."

"Yeah. I'm just new here."

"It doesn't matter. People will rally around you anyway. And your grandma is not new. And you know how small towns are. You're related to her, so they're gonna love you no matter what."

"True." She sighed. "I wish I could have figured out how to make bread as good as hers. I have a feeling I'm never going to learn."

"I wouldn't say that. It might not be just like hers, but you'll figure something out. And plus, maybe the new meds will help her, and you'll have months and months together, if not years. The doctor doesn't always have to be right."

"I like the way you think, but I guess I kind of feel like after watching her the last couple of days, she's gone downhill so fast. On the one hand, I kind of hope that she just slips away really quickly and easily and doesn't suffer. It sounded to me like it could end up being really painful."

"I think that's probably the thing that I would want to focus on. Making sure that she's comfortable."

"That's the one thing she said, and I felt like it was the only thing she was afraid of. She actually seemed happy after the diagnosis. Like she was excited to go see Jesus and her parents and her son who had died and her husband. Just...full of peace and joy. But she did ask the doctor and specify that she didn't want to be in pain."

Claire sat there for a moment, her eyes cast down, thinking.

He let her be alone with her thoughts and gave her the time that she needed. He didn't want to intrude. She might not have a whole lot of time to sit and try to process. And that last visit with Grandma would probably be something that she would revisit over and over, particularly if it ended up being the very last visit. And especially if Grandma went as quickly as what Claire seemed to be afraid she was going to.

Finally, after a bit, she said, "Well. I probably ought to go back in. I think I'm going to leave the house painting and the kitchen and all of the other things to you. I'll probably just sit with Grandma."

"If you need a break, you be sure to ask me."

"I will. Although I expect we'll be inundated with family who want to say their goodbyes to her. I know I would want to."

He thought she might be surprised. Sometimes people could be really weird when death was involved and would do anything to avoid it. But maybe she would be pleasantly surprised. It seemed like Claire was hoping that people would come anyway. Maybe for Grandma's sake.

"Thanks for sharing with me. I will let you know if I get Grace's number, and I'll be expecting to spend the evening either here or at the school tomorrow."

"Thanks. I'll keep you apprised of everything that's going on."

"Sounds good."

They stood together, and their arms brushed. It was an accident, at least on his part, and he expected her to jerk away. But she didn't.

Instead, she looked up at him, as though she was going to say something, but she ended up just staring into his eyes.

It was only for a second or two, but it felt like an eternity to him.

Maybe there was something a little more between them. He felt an odd sensation between his heart and his ribs, something warm and swirly, and he wasn't sure exactly what that meant.

Other than he wanted to move closer, put his hand up to cup her cheek, put his arms around her, and give her strength. Somehow help her be strong for the days and weeks ahead.

"Thanks," she whispered again, and then she turned and started to hurry away.

"Hey," he said, and she stopped right away.

"Yeah?"

"Would you take my glass, please?" He was walking toward her and handing it to her.

"Sure. Sorry." She laughed a little self-consciously and reached out for his glass. Their fingers brushed, and his eyes held hers as they did. He wasn't sure whether she felt the sensation that crawled up his arm and seemed to go the whole way down to his toes, but it made him want to close his eyes.

Instead, he said so softly it was almost a whisper, "Thank you."

He wasn't even sure what he was thanking her for. Taking his glass, he supposed, but she just nodded and then curled her fingers around the glass before she turned and hurried away.

What terrible timing on his part. She had an ex she was dealing with, was going to be separated from her children for the first time, a grandma who was dying, potential family members descending upon her, and a limited amount of time in which to get all the things done that she needed to do, juggling her children and her grandma and hospice and doctors' appointments and new medicine, and there he was, thinking that maybe he was falling in love with her.

Sixteen

C laire looked around. The cabinets had been removed; there were plates and cups in various spots all over the house. She couldn't give Josiah a hard time for taking such a long time to get things done, since he was trying to get the outside of the house finished on the nice days and working on the kitchen when it rained or was cold.

They had known that this was going to happen with Grandma. But beyond that, she was bone-tired. It had been quite a day, from the doctor's appointment to the family phone calls she had had to make, where she'd given each person the news that Grandma was dying, and soon.

Everyone had been surprised, no one had expected it, but at the same time, there weren't a whole lot of people who seemed like they were going to drop everything and come say goodbye.

Claire had been shocked. Until she had thought about it and realized that if she weren't here, she might not come. As much as she would want to see Grandma one more time, it was death. She didn't want to deal with death. She didn't want to see it, didn't want to be around it. She wanted to remember Grandma as happy and energetic and fun, always with a cup of tea in one hand and a plate of cookies in the other. Or her kitchen smelling of warm, fresh-baked bread. She didn't want to remember her as an old lady lying in bed, too tired to get up to even go to the bathroom.

She had talked to hospice—they were coming in the morning for a consultation. She didn't even know whether Grandma would be able to get up or not. She supposed hospice had seen people go downhill that quickly.

When she'd talked to Grandma earlier, she was insistent that she would be able to attend the children's end-of-year program. But after Claire had struggled to get her awake enough to go to the bathroom and get her clothes changed, and had to help her with all of it, she could hardly see how Grandma could attend a program the next night.

It wasn't like a good night's sleep was going to make her better.

They had gotten her pills—the prescriptions that they'd picked up before they'd come home—and figured out when she should take what and what she might need if she were in pain during the day or during the night.

It all seemed overwhelming.

Her phone buzzed, and she thought about not even looking at it. It was late enough that it was almost time for her to go to bed, and tomorrow was another day. But it might be family members letting her know that they were going to come in, and she wanted everyone to have the opportunity to see Grandma and to feel welcome. Grabbing her phone, she flipped it over and saw that it was Josiah.

I got Grace's number for you.

He sent her a contact card.

GRACE HONEA

She sighed. He'd been a rock. She remembered what they'd said about depending on people instead of depending on the Lord, but at the same time, God gave her people to lean on, and Josiah had been one of those people that she needed.

And then she thought about the way their arms had brushed earlier and then their fingers. It was almost like... She wasn't quite sure. It was weird. It wasn't the way she normally felt when she rubbed arms with someone. It was...different. But right now, she had enough on her plate, and he didn't seem the slightest bit interested in her, other than being a friend. And she felt like that was probably mostly because he liked her grandma and wanted to give her a hand any way he could.

She appreciated it, for sure, and was going to take him up on as much as she needed to, because she felt like he was sincere and truly wanted to help. But as for anything more, that was down the road. This was not the time. Not for him, and definitely not for her. Still, it really felt to her like there was something going on there. On her end anyway. And the idea of stepping into his arms and having them come around her and being able to rest her head on his chest and relax into him was almost more tempting than she could bear. She wanted to text him back and ask him if he could come over.

Where that thought came from, she had no idea, and she shoved it aside right away. She definitely was not doing that. Not only because her children were in the house, but her grandma was too, and it was almost bedtime. Not appropriate in any way.

Still, it was what she wanted to do.

Thanks. I'll give her a call.

She sent the text back and then figured she would call Grace in the morning. And then she thought, why wait? She'd made so many phone calls and done so many things today, checking everything off her list, that she figured one more thing wouldn't hurt, right?

But maybe she should wait until she had a little more energy. Maybe she wouldn't be so emotional.

Then she thought she could just send her a text and ask her to meet somewhere. Not tomorrow, because her kids had their school program. Although she could meet earlier in the day. Josiah would be there to be with her grandma. She could do it after the meeting with hospice.

Taking a breath, she held her phone in her hand, trying to talk herself into doing it. Why was it so hard?

Finally, she punched the number in, thought for a minute, wrote out a short text, and before she could chicken out, she hit send.

> Grace, this is Claire. I got your number from Josiah. Would you be able to meet tomorrow at 2 o'clock at the healing garden?

She looked around the kitchen, with the cabinets out and the countertops off and dust and dirt everywhere. It felt like a true mess.

Maybe she'd ask Josiah if he could just focus on getting the kitchen done. That way, at least they'd have a good place to cook food. And that went a long way toward making a person feel better. She had decided to go to bed when her phone beeped with a text.

She closed her eyes, trying to find strength in her soul before she opened them and looked down at her phone.

> I'd love to. See you tomorrow at two at the healing garden.

It was that easy. She'd sent a message and had a positive response. Grace didn't just say yes she would—she said she'd love to. That made her feel like Grace truly did want to renew their friendship, not demand apologies and rake her over the coals for her behavior years ago, even though it was terrible behavior that she was ashamed of now.

Before she went upstairs, she walked back to her grandma's bedroom, where she'd left the door cracked. A nightlight burned beside the bed, and Claire stuck her head in. Grandma slept peacefully.

That was good. She smiled at Grandma's even breathing, probably helped along by the pain pill she'd given her earlier. She was thankful for them, but they really had made Grandma loopy and out of it. And she hated that.

Still, the pain was the thing Grandma had been concerned about, and Claire was happy that they were able to ease it.

With a last look, as the sheet slowly rose and fell with her grandma's breathing, she turned around and walked up the stairs to her bed.

Seventeen

The next morning, Claire got up early. She wanted to check on Grandma and do anything she needed to do with her before she got the kids up and ready for their last day of school. Their program was tonight, and they were having practices that day, plus there were little cards that they had made for their friends, since they weren't going to be seeing them all summer the way everyone else was. She knew her kids felt a little left out, and she felt like Lana, especially, would have preferred to stay home.

She was only thirteen, and Claire would have to check the laws of Massachusetts, but she was pretty sure that once Lana turned fourteen, she could decide if she would like to stay with one parent full-time.

Claire wasn't sure how she felt about that or whether she would even suggest that to Lana. She would love to have Lana with her all summer, but it wouldn't be fair to Ted, who, despite all his flaws, she believed truly did love his children. Just not enough to keep him on the straight and narrow. The love he had for her wasn't enough either.

That didn't mean there was something wrong with her or wrong with the kids. It meant there was something wrong with Ted.

It had taken her a long time to figure that out and even longer to believe it, and even now, she wasn't sure she was totally on board with the whole idea.

She felt like she hadn't been enough.

She thought she was over that, and she shook her head, getting dressed and combing her hair, trying to do it quietly so she didn't wake the kids up before it was necessary. One last day, and then tomorrow they could sleep in. She always allowed them a whole week to sleep in after school was out before she started making them get up and work a little bit in the morning. Her mom had always said that it was important that kids learn to work, and she didn't think it was right for children to lie around in bed.

Her mom, now living in New Mexico, hadn't thought she would be able to make it out to see her own mom anytime soon. But she had said she would look into flights.

Her mom's brother, Uncle Bob, who lived in Nebraska, had sounded like he was going to try to make the trip—he just didn't know when.

Grandma had a few other kids, and some grandkids, and Claire had called them all. But she didn't have any solid dates for any of them to come visit.

Grandma had been disappointed but tried to hide it.

Still, Claire picked up her phone, hoping that maybe a few texts had come in overnight.

Nothing, except something from Josiah from earlier, telling her that he was taking care of his mom but that he'd be over as soon as possible and to let him know if she needed him to bring anything.

She appreciated the thought and the consideration, and thought about it for a moment before she texted back and told him thanks, but there was nothing right now.

She was still smiling at the fact that someone had been kind enough to check on her as she walked downstairs and decided to put water on the stove before she went in to wake up Grandma.

She wasn't actually going to wake her grandma. She was going to go in and check and see if she was awake, and if she wasn't, she would let her grandma sleep until she was ready to wake up.

Or maybe until shortly before the meeting with hospice.

She didn't know. She was new at this. She didn't know what to do.

She didn't know how long her grandma might sleep. Maybe the pills would keep her in bed all day. The pharmacist had said that different people had different reactions to them.

Regardless, the door was still partially cracked, and she peeked in before she pushed it open any farther.

Grandma lay peacefully there, just the way she'd been last night when Claire had checked on her. It looked like she hadn't moved at all.

And then Claire realized she wasn't moving at all. She wasn't even breathing.

Something gripped her entire chest and pulled it tight and hard and hot as she pushed the door open and hurried to the bed.

"Grandma? Grandma?" She spoke the first word softly and then louder, and then she practically yelled, "Grandma!"

She touched the body, but it was cool and hard, and she drew her hand back immediately. There was no question. Her grandma had stepped into heaven.

Leaving Claire and the children and the rest of the family here behind.

It was graduation, promotion, a happy day, except it didn't feel like that to Claire. It felt heavy and hard and sad and like she wasn't nearly prepared. She thought she was going to have more time. She thought she was going to be able to talk to her grandma about more things. Make more bread together, watch the flowers grow, spend the summer together. Grandma could comfort her as she cried over the fact that her kids were gone and her family was broken up and she didn't know what she was going to do with the rest of her life. But life looked bleak and empty now, and her kids hadn't even left yet. Just Grandma.

She sat down in the chair beside the bed, staring at the body. Did she need to move the sheet to cover her head? Wasn't that what people did? Why did they do that? Was it something she had to do? Grandma just looked like she was sleeping. And then... What did one do when one found a dead body in their house in the morning? She assumed hospice was going to go over all that with her. Or someone was. She had no idea what to do. Did you call the police? An ambulance? Who?

She had no idea. She'd never felt so helpless and alone, so very, very alone, in her life before.

Her phone—she still held her phone in her hand, and she looked at it. Who to call? What to do?

And then she thought, Josiah. He was on his way over anyway. Maybe he could come faster and stand beside her while she tried to figure this all out. She wasn't going to be arrested for killing her grandma, was she? Like...people would understand her grandma was dying and it had nothing to do with her, right? Was she going to be in trouble?

She was going to text Josiah, but with those thoughts, she decided to call him instead. And then, after she dialed his number and the phone had rung once, she wondered if the police would look at her phone and see that her first call had not been to 911 or the police or to some kind of authority, but to someone else. Maybe they would accuse her of trying to get rid of the body so that she could get rid of the evidence.

She tried to calm herself down and remind herself that her grandma had cancer—they were expecting her to die. No one was going to blame her or think that she'd killed her.

Wait. Did she give her an overdose of her pills last night? Because she wasn't supposed to die so fast, was she? Except the doctor had said she could die in her sleep tonight.

That was what had happened.

"Hello?"

"I didn't kill her. I promise. I gave her the exact amount of pills that I was supposed to, and when I checked on her before I went to bed, she was fine, and I woke up this morning, and she's just lying there, and I thought she was sleeping, but she's not sleeping—she's dead—and I'm afraid I'm going to go to jail for the rest of my life!" By the time she was done, she was practically shouting and sobbing and almost incoherent, but Josiah sounded calm and controlled when he spoke.

"Claire. She had cancer. Everyone knew she was going to die. I'll be there in five minutes. Stay on the phone with me. You don't need to do anything until I'm there."

"I can't leave her alone. I was supposed to watch her. Am I going to get arrested?"

"No. You're not going to get arrested."

"But who do I call? Do I call the police? Do I call an ambulance? She doesn't need an ambulance. They're not going to resuscitate her. She was hard. I touched her—she was cold. It was terrible."

"Claire. It's okay. They're not going to arrest you. I promise."

"How can you promise? You don't know."

"I do know. I actually know the head of the police personally, and he's a reasonable guy. We'll have your doctor talk to them if necessary. She just told you yesterday she could die in her sleep tonight. And that's what she did."

"But I didn't believe her. I didn't actually think it was going to happen. I thought I had all summer."

She hadn't cried yet. But to her dismay, tears were streaming down her face, and she broke down in sobs.

"I'm sorry. I thought I was ready for this. I mean, I knew I wasn't. But I knew she was going to die."

"It's okay. It's normal for you to be upset. No one expects you not to be upset. That would be weird."

"What? I want to be calm. I want to be in control. But I'm just... overwhelmed."

"'When my heart is overwhelmed: lead me to the rock that is higher than I.'" He quoted the Bible verse.

His words, the familiar Psalm, the calm tone, the knowledge that someone was coming to stand beside her, calmed her and eased her mind.

And then a new thought struck. "I should have been there. I should have been sitting beside her, holding her hand. She died alone."

"She didn't die alone. Jesus promises to walk with us through the valley of death. He was there with her. She didn't need you. Why would she want you when she had Jesus?"

It might have sounded like Josiah was telling her she wasn't loved, but Claire knew exactly what he was saying. He was telling her that her time to hold her grandma was over, and Jesus took over from there. Who would want a human when they could have Jesus?

And he was right.

Thankfully, it didn't take him long to get there. As soon as she saw his truck pulling in, she hung up and ran to the front steps and met him as he parked.

He opened the door, and she rushed into his arms, not thinking that it was inappropriate at all, just knowing that she needed some kind of comfort, and he was there, and she was going to take whatever he was willing to give her.

"Hey. It's okay. I know this is hard, but you're going to do it. I'll be here with you. We'll do it together." He stroked her hair and held her against his chest, feeling so warm and hard and solid and alive. So alive. Her grandma wasn't. Gone. Gone from this world, and she felt lonely and left behind and afraid.

This is where she was supposed to cling to Jesus, but Jesus had given her people to cling to as well.

"I don't want to put you in the place of Jesus, but it feels so good to have someone alive to hold onto."

"I'm here to hold onto as long as you need me," he said, his words reassuring and calm and with that same easy, confident tone that he'd been using on her all morning since she'd called him, and it infused her with strength and with determination that she could do this.

"I don't want to go to jail," she said.

"You're not going to jail." He didn't laugh, and she appreciated it, and he smoothed his hand over her hair at the same time, making her feel reassured.

"It kind of sounds like I'm more upset about going to jail than I am about my grandma dying, but I just don't want to die in jail. Also, I've never been in a house by myself with a dead person." She paused for a moment, then she said, "Oh my goodness. The kids! They've got to get to school. It's the last day. What can we do? Should I tell them about Grandma?"

"I don't think that you need to tell them. They have to get through the school day. Can you shut the door and get them off to school?"

That sounded reasonable to her. She would rather tell them after they came home, even if they didn't make it to their program that night. At least they'd made it through the last day of school.

They'd had enough upheaval in their life. They didn't need more today.

"All right. I'm not sure it's the right decision, but I'm going to shut the door, and I'm not going to tell them about her until tonight when they get home. Then I'll make a decision about whether or not we go to the program."

She closed her eyes, not wanting to let go of his solid strength. Then her eyes flew open, and she drew back. "I texted Grace last night and told her that I would meet her at two today. I can't. I can't do that. And I have to cancel hospice and figure everything else out."

He put a hand on top of her head, running down her hair, and put his thumb over her lips.

"Shhh. One thing at a time. We'll get the kids off to school. Then we'll start making phone calls. If you need help, I'll make phone calls too. We'll figure it out. Let's get the kids to school first."

"All right. Kids to school. Do you think I should call the authorities? Who do I call?"

"Actually, I'm not exactly sure who to call. Maybe a funeral home. You don't need an ambulance, and there's no point in bringing one out here. I can get on the phone with the funeral home and stand outside and talk while you take care of the kids if you want. I can ask if I need to call an ambulance or if they're going to send the coroner to pronounce her dead or what. I'll try to make sure that we don't have anyone in the house until the kids leave. What time would that be?"

She appreciated his calmness again. His willingness to take on some undesirable task, because she sure as shooting didn't want to have to call the coroner. Or the funeral home.

"Do you know if your grandma had a certain funeral home?"

"I don't. But there's only one in Blueberry Beach, and there's none in Strawberry Sands or Raspberry Ridge. I think that's the closest."

"Then I'll get a hold of them. Okay?"

"Yeah. I'll go in, shut the door, get the kids up." She looked at her watch and then told him what time they needed to be on the bus. Then she realized that was only twenty-five minutes away and jerked away from him. "I need to run. I didn't realize it was only twenty-five minutes. Lana is going to die."

"Maybe she's already up getting herself ready."

That was so absurd, Claire actually laughed.

"How do you have me laughing? My grandma died, I'm a mess, and I'm out here laughing with you." She put her hands down, and she turned to him fully and went back and gave him a hug. "Thank you. Thank you so much. I really, really can't tell you how much I appreciate you just being here."

"I'm here. I'm staying as long as you need. Okay?"

She leaned back, looked up at his eyes, and nodded. "Thanks."

Eighteen

"Yes, the funeral will be on Saturday, with the viewing in the morning from nine to twelve, and the funeral will be at twelve. There will be a meal provided by the church in Raspberry Ridge."

"Yes. I can text you directions if you want me to."

"Okay. Thanks."

Claire hung up. That was the last phone call she had to make.

"How many said they're going to try to make it?" Josiah said, sounding as steady as ever but looking a little tired. It was 1:30 in the afternoon, and it had already been quite a day. Josiah had taken care of the arrangements for the body, and to Claire's everlasting relief, no one had questioned anything. It was just accepted that a woman with cancer who was expected to die had died.

Grandma had died.

She'd been so scared that she was going to get in trouble. She hadn't done anything wrong. Still, Josiah had taken care of all of it, and her grandma was at the funeral home now, where they would prepare her for burial.

Josiah had been the one who had found the burial plot that Grandma had at the little church in Raspberry Ridge just outside of town. Claire had even forgotten the church existed. But Grandma had a plot, and the funeral home had taken care of contacting the gravediggers.

They didn't need to have an actual grave ready until Saturday, when they would have a short graveside service after the funeral.

Josiah had helped her figure all that out too.

She'd been leaning toward cremation, but Grandma hadn't said one way or the other, and since she had the burial plot, it seemed to make more sense to do it that way. Grandma had money saved, and Josiah had found that in her desk as well while Claire had been busy calling all the relatives that she had just called the day prior.

Her mom was coming up from New Mexico, which was nice, except she wasn't going to stay very long. She needed to get back, because her husband's mother wasn't well, and she was responsible for taking care of her.

It made Claire a little bit angry that her mom was more concerned about her mother-in-law and was shirking her duty in favor of taking care of her husband's mom. But Claire supposed that was how life went. The living demanded more attention than the dead anyway. She didn't know her stepfather and had never met his mother. Maybe she was a sweet lady who deserved her mother's loyalty.

"So now all we have to do is wait for the kids to come home and we'll tell them, and then they can make the decision as to whether they still want to go to their program or not."

"I feel like we should call the school and warn them that the kids might not be there."

"I think they'll understand, but if you want to call the school, you certainly can." His voice was easy, calm, and rational.

"All right. I think I'll wait."

And then she remembered. Grace!

"I never canceled with Grace," she said, frantically picking her phone up and looking for her number.

"What time were you supposed to meet her?" Josiah asked as she dug through her contacts before her fingers froze.

"I couldn't possibly—" She broke off. Why not? She had time. She had several hours. Her children got out of school at three o'clock, but by the time the bus brought them back, it was closer to four.

Sometimes she would pick them up just to give them a little bit more time at home.

"I wouldn't have very long to talk to her."

"It might be nice to have someone to talk to," Josiah suggested.

"Other than you?" she asked, because he had been the one she had needed to talk to all day.

"I can go with you if you want me to. Or," he looked at the kitchen behind her, "I can work on the kitchen a bit. I am sorry that the house is such a disaster during this time."

"It's not your fault. It's mine for starting the outside and then making you have to finish it."

"I don't mind. I just feel bad that I couldn't get it done faster."

"It is what it is. We can't change it now." She couldn't believe she was saying that. The Claire of a few weeks ago would obsess over the state of the house, but the Claire of right now didn't care. She wasn't sure if it was just numbness from the grief that would explode upon her at some point when she wasn't aware, or whether it was a true calm and peace from the Lord.

One thing she knew for sure—it was good to have Josiah beside her. His steady, calm presence had bolstered her throughout the day.

"All right. You're right. Why not go meet with Grace?" And then she nodded her head. "I know I'm going to be more emotional, but it was going to be an emotional meeting anyway."

"All right. I can seriously go if you think you're going to need me."

"No. Grace isn't going to hurt me. I know that now. And while I'm a little bit nervous, I'm actually kind of excited to talk to her. She was my best friend back in the day. We did everything together."

"Yeah, I remember you two were inseparable. A lot of times, you wore the same outfits to school and styled your hair the same. People called you twins."

"We often wished we had been twins. We preferred each other over anyone in our families."

How had they gotten to be so far apart when they had been so close at one time?

She couldn't answer that, and she really didn't know, and she supposed it didn't matter now anyway.

"Should I change?" she asked, looking down at the outfit that she'd put on this morning and never changed. Jeans and T-shirt and tennis shoes.

"You're asking the wrong person. This is one thing I can't help you with. I can tell you that it's clean. And if I owned a restaurant, I wouldn't kick you out."

"All right. That's good enough." She smiled at him and knew that she owed him more than she'd ever be able to repay. "Thanks again. Help yourself to whatever's in the kitchen. Sorry there's no fresh bread."

"No problem. I'll work on getting more stuff cleaned out and see what I can get done before you get back." And then he said, "And don't worry about getting back here before your kids. If you're not, I'll handle things until you arrive. I won't tell them about Grandma."

"All right. I'll do my best to get back, but thanks for the reassurance that you've got things under control."

She walked out the door, humming to herself. How could she be humming on the day Grandma died? But she was. She found she was humming an old, upbeat hymn. One that talked about depending on the Lord and going to Him when she had a problem.

It was perfect for today, and she smiled, though she wasn't sure why it had popped into her head, because she hadn't thought about it in years.

Some of the old hymns were the best. And then she smiled softly to herself. She was glad to be back in Raspberry Ridge and going to a church that sang hymns and preached from the Bible. She had a feeling she was going to need it in the weeks and months to come.

It didn't take long to get into town, and she was early as she pulled into the healing garden, but there was a car already there. She wasn't sure whether it was Grace's car or not.

She got out and walked through the gate.

Josiah had told her to follow the path back—there was a pretty waterfall and a soothing reflection pond. She found it easily and thought that Grace was already there.

"Grace?" she asked, pretty sure it was her friend.

The woman turned, and then her face broke into a smile. "Claire!"

She moved forward, her arms out. If Claire had wondered how the reunion would go, she needn't have worried. Grace embraced her like a long-lost friend. And she supposed she was exactly that.

"Thank you so much for being willing to meet me."

"I should thank you," Claire said.

Grace paused. "I heard about your grandma."

"Oh good. I thought I was going to have to tell you, and... I told so many people today, I really didn't want to have to go through it again."

"You don't have to. I'm not sure exactly how everything went, but I think it had something to do with my mom talking to Josiah's mom, who knows the funeral director's aunt, and yeah. Small towns."

Grace grinned, and Claire laughed. "I know I'm supposed to be sad, but I've laughed some today too, which I think is weird."

"Laughter is a stress relief, just like crying or anything else. In my personal opinion, I prefer laughing to crying, and I'll do that any day."

"I never thought about it like that. Do you really think that laughter lets stress out just like crying does?"

"I don't know, but I always feel better after I've laughed. And somehow, when things are sad or hard, I always do better if I'm laughing." She lifted her hands and shrugged her shoulders. "I don't know if I'm handling it well or if I'm doing it in some kind of unhealthy way. But it works for me."

"I suppose that's the thing that matters."

Grace nodded. "Would you like to sit down? I always find this spot the most comforting of all the spots in the garden."

"Yeah. Vera and her husband did an amazing job on this."

"They're professionals. And you can tell. I think, since they dedicated it to their son, they spared no expense."

"They dedicated it to their son? I thought they had a whole bunch of kids. Did they lose one?" She seemed to remember a bunch of kids running around the church after Vera and Dominic. Or maybe it was Dominic and Vera running around after the kids. That picture seemed more accurate.

"Before they had those children, they had one that they doted on, an only child. They lost him to a sudden fever, I think. Anyway, this garden was dedicated to him. They almost separated, but when they built it, they ended up coming back together. And then God blessed them with a whole pile of children."

"Wow. That's quite a story."

"It is. It's a beautiful love story. They should write it in a book sometime."

The two friends smiled, and then Claire took a breath. "I need to apologize."

"Not to me. That's not what I wanted to meet about." Grace shook her head and put up a hand.

Claire took her hand and placed it over Grace's, clutching it and holding it in her lap.

"Let me. I was unkind and unfair to you when we were in high school. And I should have apologized long before this. I gave you a hard time about Trevor. I said you stole him from me. It wasn't the slightest bit true. Everyone, including me, knew that Trevor had a thing for you. I didn't even really like him that much. I just...wanted there to be some kind of contention between us, because after...Yolanda died—" She had paused before saying Yolanda's name. It still didn't roll off her tongue very well. Grace flinched as well. But this was one of the things that she needed to get through. "—I wanted to put distance between us. Being with you reminded me of the accident. And no matter how much time went by, I still felt guilty and bad. And every time I was with you, it just made it worse. Especially during the summer when we were out by the lake."

"I felt the same way."

"I'm sorry I didn't realize. I was just looking for an excuse not to talk to you. It was childish and dumb, but it accomplished what I wanted it to. We didn't talk for the whole last year."

"And then I broke up with Trevor because I missed you."

"I'm sorry. You should have been together and gotten married." She paused and then furrowed her brow. "You're engaged?"

Grace smiled and nodded, obviously happy. "We are. I was stubborn. I was determined I was going to make something of myself. It's true that I broke up with Trevor partly because of you, but it was also because I wanted to leave this town. I wanted to show everyone that I could make something of myself, and for some reason, to me, success meant going to the city and making a lot of money. So I got a good job, married a successful man, and I had it all before I lost everything. They just repossessed my car last week. Finally."

"Ouch. Sorry."

"It was a blessing and a relief. I mean, BMWs are nice—I'm not gonna lie. But the load of debt that I was under was just smothering. And my husband cheated on me and made me feel like I was worthless."

"I know the feeling," Claire said, knowing there was something else that she and Grace could relate about.

"You were married?"

"Yes. To a lawyer, and we have two children. He cheated on me, apologized, and we went to therapy, but then he had an affair with the therapist, and that's when I said enough."

"Wow. He sounds like a piece of work."

"Yeah. But he does love the children. I think, anyway. I have them one more week, and then they go to Boston for the summer. It's going to be hard, because I've never been separated from them before."

"We have to do lots of things together this summer. I would imagine that it's even more difficult because of losing your grandma. You probably were looking forward to summer with her."

"Yeah. This all happened so suddenly. I just found out she had leukemia, and now she's gone. And you're right. I thought we had the summer to get reacquainted. But...we don't. Obviously."

"I hear through the grapevine that there might be something between you and Josiah. Remember that kiss?" Grace grinned and dipped her head forward, knocking her shoulder against Claire's.

"Oh goodness. You didn't tell anyone, did you?"

"No. But there were a lot of people there. I'm not the only one who knows about it."

"You're the only one who knows how I truly felt about it."

"That he was dreamy?"

"Don't say that. It was a...really nice kiss, but I didn't ever tell him that. I let him think that I didn't enjoy it at all."

"It was your first kiss. We talked about that for years afterward."

"That might be a little bit of an exaggeration, but...yeah." She grinned, remembering how they'd lain in bed at night talking about

Josiah and how she hadn't expected the kiss to be that nice, and whether or not she should try to strike up a relationship with him. They'd gone back and forth but eventually decided not to, and she couldn't even remember why. Some stupid teenage reason, probably.

"You know, Josiah would have been a much better choice than what I did by running off and finding a big-city lawyer to get married to. I wish I could remember now why I decided that Josiah wasn't the right guy for me, even though he was good at kissing."

"I wonder that sometimes too. I wish Trevor and I wouldn't have broken up, and I wish I wouldn't have left the way I did. But don't you think everything that we went through helped us to become the people that we are now? If we hadn't left, if we hadn't learned what we did, do you think we'd be talking here now?"

"I don't know. Maybe not. Maybe we'd still hate each other."

"I know that after the pain I went through, it shaped me into a much more compassionate, kind person who is interested in other people rather than just a narcissist."

"Yeah. I can definitely tell you the things that I've been going through have changed me. I was much more interested in being with my grandma. Although it kind of makes you wonder why God ripped her away from me just as I was interested in getting to know her again."

"That's just another pain that will shape you and mold you into somebody that is better than the person you used to be."

"I guess I'll take your word for that."

"You can. I'm sure of it."

"I'm sorry I'm probably not going to be a very good friend. I...have a lot going on. I don't know if you know that Grandma's house is in shambles, because I started painting the outside, and Josiah's ripped the kitchen apart to put in new cabinets and redo it, and everything is scattered everywhere. And... I don't know. I'll probably be depressed after my kids leave."

"It's okay. I've been depressed before. And I think the best remedy for depression is to get out and hang out with someone fun. That would be me," Grace said, winking, as though she knew she was being a little bit goofy.

"I see. You are the remedy for my depression. Gotcha."

"Seriously. I really would like to spend time with you this summer. Are you back to stay?"

"I'm not sure. I...probably will need a job. I have to go through what Grandma did with her will. But she told me she left me the farm and farmhouse and enough money to finish fixing it up. But all of her other money was divided amongst all of her other grandchildren. I have a subscription website that makes me a couple hundred dollars a month, but that's not going to be enough to keep me going. I do get some money from my ex-husband for the kids, and so far, it's been dependable. I suppose I should just assume that he's going to do what he says, but given my experience..."

"Totally understand. Even if he does do what he says he's going to do with child support, it's so hard to shove aside the fact that he didn't do what he said he was going to do with his marriage vows."

"Exactly." She felt like Grace really understood her. Especially when it came to her ex. "You didn't have children?"

"I wanted them so badly, but my ex said no. I'm so glad he did. Otherwise, it would make it so much harder."

Claire could agree enthusiastically with that. "Absolutely. It's hard enough for you to go through your husband ditching you like yesterday's trash, but to watch your children suffer—it's so, so hard. And then it's really hard to encourage your kids to be kind to him and like him and not to tell them all the bad things that he's ever done to you. I wanted to turn them against him, but I knew that wasn't the right thing to do. It was...exceptionally difficult and sometimes still is."

"I can only imagine. God was good to me there. But on the other hand, Trevor and I have already talked about it, and we want to have children. I think we're going to try for children right away."

"Are you getting married soon?"

"Yeah. Our parents just got married not that long ago, and we kind of wanted to give them their own honeymoon time. But actually, we were talking about in the next couple of weeks just going to the preacher and having our parents as witnesses. We thought we might have a get-together after church on Sunday to celebrate. Kind of like a wedding reception, only low-key and no stress."

"I love the idea of no stress." She had to admit that the idea of not stressing was a good one. And she was glad that the last things that her grandmother had talked to her about were some of the ways that she could keep from stressing—by being humble, by not having high expectations of what everyone else should do and be, by not being offended and not allowing herself to be offended over anything, by determining beforehand that she wasn't going to take anything personally.

"I better get back. My children are coming home from school, and they don't know about Grandma yet. Not unless someone on the bus told them."

"I hope no one did. I do know that word has gotten around. If I know, and you and I haven't talked in ages, then a lot of people know."

"Well, hopefully they're going to allow me to tell them. But I guess if not, I'll handle that too."

"I think we find, as we live, that we can handle a lot more than we thought we could. And that Jesus is with us every step of the way."

"Amen." They stood together and embraced.

"Thanks again for meeting me."

"I really am sorry about what I did in high school and for not responding to your messages now too. We could have talked weeks ago if I had responded and answered you."

"God's timing." Grace smiled, and it was obvious to Claire that there were no hard feelings. She did truly appreciate that.

"Let's stay in touch," Grace said as she put her arm through Claire's, and they walked down the path together.

"Absolutely." And she had every intention of keeping her word.

Nineteen

Josiah looked up as the front door opened. He wanted to get the house finished for Claire. He hated that it was such a mess while she was going through such a hard time. He couldn't imagine that the state of the house made things any easier for her. But in order to finish the kitchen, it was going to have to get worse before it got better, since he would have to take everything out in order to put things in. And it was going to take a little while, especially with the tile backsplash behind the counter and the fact that all the walls needed to be painted.

"We're home," Claire said, coming into the kitchen. She looked like she'd had quite a day, which of course he knew she had. But she had a certain glow about her, and he suspected that her talk with Grace had gone very well.

She nodded and smiled, as though she'd read his mind. "You were right. It went much better than I thought it was going to."

"What did you want to tell us, Mom?" Lana said, setting her bookbag down on a chair at the kitchen table and turning to face her mom.

"Dan, come in here. I want you to hear this too." She waited until Dan had come in. Josiah wanted to ask if he should leave. He didn't know if he should go back to work or stand there and support her or what. He waited for some kind of sign from her.

She glanced at him, and the look she gave him made him feel like she was depending on him to stand beside her. So he put his tools down, wiped his hands on the rag he carried in his back pocket, and stayed where he was. He didn't want the children to get the idea that he was somehow in partnership with their mom. It was a position that wasn't his, and he didn't want to overstep.

"You know that Grandma had cancer," Claire began.

The kids nodded, both of their faces scrunched up like they didn't understand what was going on.

"She passed away today. Her body is at the funeral home, and the funeral will be Saturday."

"Grandma died?" Lana asked immediately, sounding offended, like Grandma wasn't allowed to die without her permission.

Josiah did not allow his lips to twitch up. It wasn't exactly the reaction he was looking for. He was sure that Claire was probably befuddled by that one as well.

"Yes. The doctor had told us that it could be anytime in the next six months."

"I thought she had six months," Lana said. "I thought we'd see her when we got back from Boston at the end of the summer."

"I really thought so too. I didn't realize it was going to be so quick. But the doctor told us right there in the patient room that she wasn't God. She couldn't tell us exactly when—she just knew it was close."

"Does this mean we're not getting any more bread?" Dan asked, and again, Josiah had to keep his lips from twitching up. Dan was male through and through. Food was the most important thing.

"Well, Grandma was teaching me how to make bread."

"But yours isn't as good."

And honest. He hadn't yet learned that sometimes it was better to keep his mouth closed on occasion and that he should not say everything that was in one's head.

He supposed that was a skill that came with age and time. One that he maybe still hadn't mastered.

"I know this is sudden and unexpected. And however you're feeling, it's okay. There isn't a certain way you have to feel. Maybe you're not sad at all. We didn't know her very well."

"Yeah. I'm a little bit bummed, but... I think the bread is the thing I'm going to miss the most," Lana said, shrugging her shoulders and acting like it was no big deal.

Josiah watched Claire carefully. He didn't want her to be upset that her children weren't devastated. Stranger things had happened. And she was already in a delicate spot, at least from his point of view, although he figured Claire was probably a lot stronger than she looked.

"That's fine. I didn't have anything else I wanted to say to you. You can go play until around five, when you'll need to come in to get ready to go to your program tonight."

"We can go outside?" Dan asked, as though to make sure.

"Yes. I'll have food ready at five, and we'll get ready to go."

"Is Josiah coming with us?" Lana asked, glancing over to where he stood leaning against the counter.

"He's welcome to if he wants. He's helped me a good bit today with all the phone calls and things I needed to make. I appreciated him being here to support me so I didn't have to do everything alone."

Lana jerked her head in a nod and didn't make a comment, either positive or negative. Josiah wasn't sure exactly what she thought of him.

Not that it mattered. Once he was done doing all the things that Grandma had already paid for in the house, he probably wouldn't see Claire and her family much at all.

The thought made him feel down, like gravity had somehow gotten stronger all of a sudden.

"I'm here if you need to talk," Claire said, and her children filed out of the kitchen. Somber, but not sad or devastated. There were no tears, and there was no unbearable grief.

She waited until their footsteps had faded on the steps before she turned to him. "It was easier than I thought it was going to be. Almost too easy. But thanks for being here."

"Of course. Same way you said you're there for your kids—I'm here for you if you need anything."

The knowledge shone in her eyes. "Thank you. And thank you

again for insisting I go see Grace. It was the best decision I could have made. She'll be someone to stand by me as well."

For some reason, instead of being completely happy about that, there was a small slice of him that was a little jealous. She had someone else to lean on other than just him. He knew how selfish that was. She needed as many people as she could gather around her to help her through this time, and who was he to be the slightest bit upset? Yet he wanted to be the one she turned to. Not Grace, not someone else. Him.

That was selfish and wrong of him, and while he couldn't change his feelings that second, he certainly wasn't going to act on them. He was going to support her finding as much support for herself as she could. And he was going to graciously stand back and allow anyone else to stand beside her who wanted to, although, if she wanted him, he would be there. No questions asked.

"I'm glad you talked to her. I'm glad things turned out so well."

"I was thinking. Grandma wouldn't want us to be sad. She wouldn't want us to be upset or mope around. In fact, when she got the diagnosis from the doctor, she was happy. I want to be happy too. I want to spend the next week with my children doing all the things that we're not going to get to do all summer. Packing a whole summer's worth of things into the next week."

"I think your gram would be all on board for that. As long as there's lots of homemade bread to go along with it." He added that last part as a bit of humor, and it worked, because she laughed. He felt like this idea that she had was a good one—to be happy rather than sad. To go out of her way to find fun things to do and to make memories with her children, the way her grandma would have wanted her to. It totally sounded like something that would make Grandma happy to him.

"I was hoping you would join us for a few things. Maybe not all. I know you need to work. And I don't want to pull you away from that, and I do want to have some special time with my children—just me and them. But...maybe a boat ride? Maybe find some kites to fly down by the beach? Or horseback riding?"

"I'm sure Rodney and Becky would allow us to ride their horses or even give us a carriage ride if you're interested in that."

"I think that would be fun. Something new. I've never had one."

"Me neither. But I know they offer them. And yeah, I'm on board for whatever. Although I had already determined that I was going to work here in the kitchen as much as I could, because I figured the kitchen being in chaos was not helping your life feel more peaceful."

"I don't know that life is supposed to feel peaceful. I mean, that's the feeling I love. It's one that I actively try to pursue, but...is that the point of life?"

He stood there for a moment. "I suppose the point of life is to give glory to Jesus in everything that we say and do."

"Yeah. And I think some people do what they want and point to the Lord, but I think the whole point is to do what God wants and point to the Lord. There's a difference."

"Yeah. Sometimes I have trouble understanding the difference."

"Me too. Still, I think it glorifies God when we're happy and at peace with the things that He's brought into our lives. Whether it's a good thing, which is obviously easy to be happy and at peace over, or a hard thing, like Grandma. So I don't want to fake it exactly, but I don't want to sit around and brood. I want to be happy that Gram's in heaven, and happy that I get a week with my kids, and happy that I have a beautiful place to live and love and raise them."

"All right. Sounds like 'the joy of the Lord is your strength.'"

She smiled at his quoting of the Old Testament verse. It was a verse that had always caught him, because he had wondered how? How was the joy of the Lord strength to someone? But it seemed like Claire was going to try to live that this week—to lean on the strength of the Lord, to find the joy of the Lord, and make it her strength.

"I was hoping that you would go with us tonight. I know that originally you were going to either help us with Grandma or stay here with her, but... Would you come?"

The way she asked, the soft whisper of her breath over the words, the way she looked at him, made him feel...like maybe they were more than friends, like she admired him, like she truly desired to be with him. It stirred something in his soul, and he had to remind himself that she had just lost her grandma. He wasn't going to take advantage of whatever vulnerable state she was in.

Although, was it taking advantage when she made the move?

Still, all she had done was ask a question, and it was an easy answer for him. "Yes. Of course. I'd love to."

"All right. Then I know that you're going to need to leave early so you can spend time with your mom."

"Yeah. I probably should pack up right now and go home and help her out, make sure everything's okay."

"And then you'll be back."

"That's right."

"That sounds good." She paused for a moment and then seemed to hesitate as she shifted. Then, with deliberate steps, she closed the distance between them and hugged him, wrapping her arms around him and putting her head on his chest. His breath froze in his lungs before his arms came up and he hugged her back, probably pulling her to him harder and tighter than what was strictly necessary. It wasn't a familiar place for her—but she felt perfect in his arms, and he wanted her there. Wanted her to stay.

"Thank you. Thank you so much. Today would have been a nightmare without you. But I'm actually in a really good place—positive and upbeat—and while anytime I think about the future it looks scary, I just remind myself that I need to focus on today, which is not scary at all. It's a happy day. A celebratory day, because Grandma is with Jesus and she's happy."

"That's very wise. It's one thing to know it, and it's another thing to be able to do it. I admire you." That was true. He felt a lot of other things other than admiration, but admiration was one that he could admit to.

"Thanks to you. If you hadn't taken the time to talk to me, and help me, and be here when I needed you, I don't know what kind of mess I would be right now." She pulled back a little, and he reluctantly loosened his grip and allowed her to. "Thank you."

He nodded, not knowing what words to say, not trusting himself to not say something that he shouldn't. She'd just had a really hard thing happen, along with an exceptionally difficult year. This wasn't the time for him to tell her that he thought he was falling in love with her and ask her to consider what that might mean for her.

He wasn't even sure what he wanted. Except maybe he wanted her to admit that she was falling for him as well.

As she stepped back, he pushed away from the counter where he was leaning and pulled the rag back out of his pocket, wiping his hands, because he needed something to do with them.

"I'll be back this evening. Call me or text me if you need me, okay? Anytime, about anything."

"Okay. And thank you. It's good to know that if I need you, you're there."

He nodded, and then, as much as he didn't want to, he left the kitchen and drove away. He wanted to stay there with her. He wanted that to be his right—where they walked through this together, all the way. But that wasn't his position right now, and he had to be okay with that. Still, a man could dream.

Twenty

"All right, bring a jacket because sometimes down by the lake the wind really makes things cool."

"Yes, Mom," Lana said with what sounded like an eye roll, although she didn't actually do it. She knew she would be in trouble for being disrespectful to her mom or for doing that.

Claire sent up a silent prayer, asking the Lord for help and also asking Him to help her not dread the coming years. If this was just a taste of what the teenage years were going to be like, she wanted to bail out now. Except she didn't. They were her children, and she was grateful for every second she got to spend with them. Which was why they were taking a carriage ride and going kite flying this afternoon.

"Is everything you packed in here?" Josiah came to the door, holding up the picnic basket she'd carefully packed that morning. It was one of the things she'd found in one of the spare rooms at her grandma's house. She hadn't gone through everything, but she'd just stood in a couple of doorways, looking and thinking and remembering the good times. The picnic basket had caught her eye, and she'd thought, why not use it? So many times, things like this got stuck in a closet somewhere and never got pulled out.

"Yes. Everything except the blanket, which I see you are carrying." She pointed to his other arm.

Josiah had been amazing. Everything that she needed. The kind of man that she really wanted standing beside her. Unlike her ex, who was never there when she needed him, who was always working late or blaming her for whatever went wrong. She couldn't even imagine trying to go through something this difficult with him. He would just bury himself in work or in affairs or whatever he did and pretend to be a good dad, putting on a show anytime people from the outside world would be looking on, but when it came right down to it, she wouldn't have had the support that she desperately needed.

That Josiah had provided.

But how did she tell him? She knew her feelings for him were deepening into something that she thought could be a relationship, but how did she tell him? How did she go from nothing to having him know that she wanted to...be with him? Have a romantic relationship? Spend the rest of her life with him? It seemed a little much.

He nodded his head at her and walked out the door, leaving her with no more answers than she'd had before. She did have a date with Grace later today. They were going to go to the café in Strawberry Sands and eat together and chat.

Claire was hoping that they would talk about the tragedy, just get it out in the open so that she could quit avoiding it in her mind. To know that Grace didn't blame her for anything, and that the way she remembered it—that it was a total and complete accident—was the way that Grace remembered it as well. If there was any responsibility she needed to shoulder, she wanted to do that as well. This seemed like a good time in her life to clean up things and make a new beginning. She supposed every ending automatically meant a new beginning. And she wanted to do this one right. She'd messed up so many of her other new beginnings—she didn't want to mess this one up. And that it was going to include Josiah, if he would allow it, was a given.

She just needed to talk to him too. Maybe she should ask him out on a date.

The idea made her stomach quiver and lurch, and she decided that perhaps she could wait until her children were gone.

Yesterday they had gone swimming, even though it had really been too cold. They'd also worked a little in the flower beds. She hadn't forced her kids to do it, but she'd talked a little bit about what her grandma had done, and Lana especially had seemed interested.

Of course, they were still taking care of the chickens, and they'd cleaned out the chicken coop, putting fresh new straw in the boxes and putting the manure in a pile beside where her grandma had always had her garden. It had gotten smaller and smaller over the years, but Claire had plans for this year. Maybe it wouldn't be the masterpiece that she remembered it being in her childhood, but... Maybe it would produce something, and growing vegetables would make her feel like she'd accomplished a little. Just like a loaf of bread, no matter how much worse than her gram's, made her feel accomplished as well.

"Come on, Dan. You have your coat?"

He held up the coat that he held in his other hand. She nodded and then was surprised when he went and put an arm around her, holding her close. She wrapped her arms around him and just hugged him without saying anything.

"I love you, Mom," he said. He was still ten years old—such a perfect age. She loved it. It was before the teenage years, but after the bumbling incompetence of childhood. It was the perfect age, in her opinion. Maybe eight to ten. Seven to eleven, something like that. And both her kids were almost completely out of it.

The thought made her sad for a moment, but she pushed that feeling aside. She could be sad later. Today, she had a carriage ride to take and kites to fly.

She grabbed the backpack that she'd put on the porch along with the duffel bag that held all their kite paraphernalia.

"I love you too, Dan. You've been awesome. Are you ready to fly kites?"

"I don't ever remember flying kites before."

Even though in Boston they were close to the ocean, it just wasn't the same. To get to the beach, to get to the harbor, they had to go through town, and it took forever. And...she just never took the time. Because it wasn't like they could do much when they were there. They had to get out of town in order to find a beach that worked. They had done that some in the summer but not nearly like she'd wanted. And they were crowded.

There was just something wild and free and beckoning about the shores of Lake Michigan.

"If you let me have those, I'll throw them in the back," Josiah said, coming back for the duffel and the backpack she carried.

"I think it's up to you—you're going to want me to let you do all the work, and I'm going to be completely worthless."

"You're definitely not completely worthless. You are the spirit behind everything. Let me be the workforce." He grinned at her, and she found herself grinning back. A silly, romantic grin, the kind that she might have given a boy in junior high or high school. Not the kind that she should be handing out as a thirty-something-year-old woman, a divorcee with two children. A lot of worldly experience under her belt. But Josiah made her feel like that high school girl, made her burdens feel not as heavy as what she imagined them to be, and made life seem like it could be fun and free and not as serious and careworn as what she always wanted to make it.

She wanted to be with someone like that. Someone who helped her be better.

They turned and walked together off the porch. The kids were already in the back of the truck, and she walked around to her side while Josiah put the duffel and the backpack in the back, along with the picnic basket and the cooler that held their drinks.

She anticipated a really nice day.

And she wasn't wrong. Rodney and Becky were awesome. They had the carriage but not hooked up, and her children watched with fascination as they showed how they cared for the horses before they hooked them up, picked their feet, and explained what they were doing as they got the carriage and all the straps and harness attached.

Claire found herself watching with fascination as well. She'd never seen anything like it. And the carriage ride was fantastic. There was just something about being pulled along by the strength of magnificent horses that lent a magical feel to the entire day.

Rodney and Becky were charming and sweet, but not overbearing, and at times, the four of them sat in the back laughing over something or pointing out ships on the horizon or interesting waves—just all the things that people saw when they were by the lake and with their family and people they loved.

Claire couldn't shake the feeling that she wished that this was her family. She wished she hadn't messed up so badly. But maybe she'd needed the mistakes in order to become who she was. Maybe without the mistakes, this day wouldn't be so bright, so beautiful, so perfect. She wouldn't understand or appreciate perfection without having gone through the pain and agony of imperfection.

The thought settled her and gave her a calmness and a rightness. And she stopped wishing that she had done things differently. Although she probably always would have that desire, she knew that God had allowed her to go down the path she was on for a specific reason, and if the timing had been different, it wouldn't have been right.

Once Rodney and Becky had taken them back to the stable and unhitched the carriage, inviting them in for a snack which they declined, they got back in the truck and headed down the beach a bit, to a deserted spot that was wide enough for them to fly kites comfortably.

Josiah showed them how to put their kites together, and they all worked at them. She could just imagine that Ted would have hired someone to put the kites together. She was surprised by the thought and then pushed it out of her head completely. She didn't want to spoil the day by thinking about Ted. He was gone. Part of her past. A part of it, but still in the past.

And she didn't want to spoil today with those thoughts. It was okay to think about becoming stronger, becoming better, even thinking about how the pain had molded and shaped her, but to think about how Ted would have done everything wrong wasn't productive at all.

They all had their kites together, and Josiah and Lana had theirs in the air while she and Dan were still working on getting theirs up. For some reason, hers just would not fly. She was about to take the tail off when Josiah came over and studied her kite for a bit as she worked, trying to get it more than ten feet in the air.

"I think you have the cross spar on backward," he finally said.

She laughed. She'd figured she'd done it wrong. She pulled her kite back down, and he pointed out that she had flipped it around and put it on the wrong side.

"That's why these things are all twisted," he said, pointing to the places where the cross spar locked in.

"I see. I guess I thought that was a weird way for it to go, but I suppose I was eager to get my kite in the air and didn't take the time to do it right."

"That's okay. That helps you learn," he said, winking at her and then moving a bit as his own kite took a dip and almost hit the water.

She thought about that. It was representative of her life. Maybe she'd been in such a rush after high school that she'd taken what looked like the easy route, eager to get her life started, when she should have paid attention and done a little better job. Again, just like Josiah had said, the detour had made her wiser. It had taught her things that she wouldn't have learned otherwise. And she had two amazing children because of it as well.

They flew kites for more than an hour, their faces bright, their smiles easy and free. Dan managed to get his kite tangled up with Lana's, which made Lana mad, but it was just one more learning experience, in Claire's eyes anyway. They stopped for lunch, spreading a blanket out and using her grandma's picnic basket, with all the goodies that she'd packed, including freshly baked bread. It wasn't warm, but the butter was soft, and she had gotten some of her grandma's raspberry jelly out of the pantry, and that made up for any lack of warmth.

It was funny how being outside worked up an appetite, and all the food they'd packed was consumed. Claire could have eaten a little more too. But it was probably good for her to not eat too much. She still was going to go meet with Grace later.

"We should do this every day," Dan said, happily shoving the last chocolate chip cookie into his mouth. It was store-bought, but maybe next time they did this, Claire would have the time to make homemade chocolate chip cookies. Hers were just as good as her grandma's, if she did say so herself.

Since her grandma seemed to be the gold standard for everything.

"I had a great day. And I'm totally down for doing it again," Josiah said. And Claire gave him a smile that she supposed said way too much about how she was feeling. His eyes widened a bit, like he was surprised by the feeling on her face, but she didn't look away. After all, this was her new beginning. She wasn't going to hide from it.

"If you hadn't tangled my kite up, I would have had a better time," Lana said. "But it was pretty fun." She smiled, and that made Claire's heart light and happy. Who knew what would be going on next year. Maybe Lana would decide she wanted to live with her dad. Maybe she would want to spend time with her friends rather than her family. Maybe something totally unexpected would have happened by then. Whatever—Claire would cherish this time. They put all their garbage back in the picnic basket to be disposed of when they got home, folded the blanket up, and flew kites for another hour or so, until they decided it was time to go home.

"I can get some wood ready and be ready to have a fire when you're back from meeting with Grace, if you think you'd like that?" Josiah asked as they pulled into the driveway, and the kids piled out.

"That would be an amazing ending to a perfect day."

"I hope your talk goes well," Josiah said, his hands on the steering wheel. He didn't move to get out.

"I wanted to do that before we took our boat ride tomorrow." Josiah had rented a boat, and they were going to go out in it for a bit. She'd kept a careful eye on the weather, and it seemed like it would be a perfect summer day. Perfect for a boat ride. Perfect for a family to spend time together.

"I think that's a good idea. Put those things in the past where they belong."

"Yeah. Make sure I'm remembering it right. I sometimes think that maybe I changed what I think happened because I don't want to take responsibility for anything that I did."

"I'm sure Grace will set you straight."

"I hope so."

"She will," Josiah said, and a hand lifted from the wheel and moved over to cover hers, which sat on the seat between them.

"I had a good time. Thank you." He looked into her eyes, his hand covering hers, her heartbeat loud and fast in her chest as her breath seemed to catch in her throat, and her mouth went dry.

"It wouldn't have been the same without you. Thank you." She wanted to say more, wanted to say a lot more, but beyond Josiah's head, she could see that Dan had run up to the window and was waiting for him to get out.

"Looks like Dan wants to talk to you."

"I'll see you later."

"Yeah," she said, jumping out of the truck and breaking the spell. She needed to get in her car and leave. They'd barely left any time for her to drive to Strawberry Sands in order to meet Grace. In hindsight, maybe she shouldn't have insisted on meeting her, but she wanted to get this behind her like she told Josiah. They were going out on the lake tomorrow, and she didn't want any clouds—any dark clouds—hanging over their day.

Twenty-One

Grace was already seated at the table when Claire walked into the cute little diner. The special was fried chicken, and Claire had to smile as she read it. She signaled to the waitress that she was going to be sitting with Grace, and the waitress nodded and said, "I'll bring a glass of iced water and get your drink order in a bit."

She nodded and walked over, sliding into the booth on the opposite side of the table and saying, "Hey there. Sorry I'm a bit late."

"No problem. I was early. On purpose. I guess you might remember that's kind of how I am." Grace grinned sheepishly, and Claire nodded. She remembered that her friend was always punctual and perfect. Although the thought used to send a little spike of jealousy buzzing through her, now it just made her smile. She loved her friend that way. And she didn't want her to change.

"You look different. Better," Grace said, sounding surprised.

"Yeah. I've gone through a lot the last 48 hours, but it's all been good things, I think. And I'm hoping that today is a good thing too."

"Same. That's the whole reason we're meeting. For me anyway. I wanted it to be good."

"I was hoping you'd be willing to talk about the tragedy. I... I'm afraid that I am not remembering correctly, and I'm afraid... I'm afraid to even think about it or talk about it or bring it up at all. I think facing it will help me face my fear and make it so that I can see it for what it is."

"I think a lot of times when we face our fears, we realize that they're not as big as what we thought they were."

"That's my hope."

"Hi, ladies. Here's your water, and the coffee that you ordered. Would you like something else to drink to go with it?" the waitress asked.

They placed their drink orders, and both of them got the special of fried chicken. The waitress nodded, telling them it was a really good choice, especially if they were looking to take some home to give to a possible marriage prospect.

Grace winked and said she'd take a box to go, but Claire, although she was tempted, did not.

"I thought you said you and Trevor are already getting married?" Claire said when the waitress left.

"There's nothing like a little extra insurance, right?" Grace said, laughing. "We decided that we were going to get married maybe in two weeks or so. And we'll have a reception at the church. We're finalizing the details, but I hope to see you at the reception."

"I'll be there. Unless something comes up. Life has been a little unpredictable lately."

"I think you have every right to say that. But I think things will settle down. We go through stages in our life, right? Where it just seems like there's turbulence everywhere we turn, and then we have smooth sailing for a while. I think God knows we need those rest periods in order to have enough strength to make it through the next turbulent time."

"I like to know that, because sometimes I feel like I can't handle any more, but... God's been so good. So many lessons, so much stuff I've realized about the old me and how I don't want the new me to be that way. Just...a lot, and it's been mostly good, although it's been a hard time, for sure." She would never say that her grandma dying had been a good time necessarily. Or an easy time. But it had been a time full of good lessons.

"Anyway. I don't want to take up all of your time. I know that when we talked, you said you only had a week with your kids. I'm sure you don't want to be gone any longer than what you need to be."

"I appreciate your consideration. You're right. Josiah is at home getting ready to have a bonfire this evening. And I promised I wouldn't be long."

"I'd like to hear about Josiah, but I think it's more important that we talk about what happened the day Yolanda died."

She thought that Grace was very deliberate in not calling it "the tragedy," as she had been, but saying Yolanda's name and saying that she died.

"It's too bad Lauren can't be here. I'm pretty sure she blames herself. I don't know exactly what happened, but she ended up not coming. And I remember Yolanda saying something about Lauren telling her to go on without her. Maybe Lauren feels like she talked Yolanda into going instead of staying, and that made a difference."

Claire thought about that for a moment and then nodded. "That makes sense. And I guess that would just add another dimension to our conversation, because it was obvious to me on that day that Yolanda wanted to be there. I don't think anyone talked her into going."

"I don't think so either." Grace nodded. "We all were excited about the trip. We were sad that Lauren wasn't there, but none of us were thinking that we wished she were there. At least, no one said anything."

"The weather was supposed to be nice," Claire started saying, trying to remember the details. "And I remember Yolanda saying that she wanted to get a tan and she didn't want to wear her life vest. We agreed, and none of us had life vests on."

"I know. I've gone back to that moment over and over again. We were so vain. It was so important to get a good tan—more important than living?" Grace shook her head. "Why? Why were we so dumb? We just...put something really stupid over something that was important. And I can't go back and change it."

"I know. I've relived that moment too. I remember her throwing her life vest down and wish that I would have just picked it up and said, 'Let's wear it for a little bit anyway.' Or something."

"Yes. Anyway, it didn't look like we would need them. The water was calm. And when we rode out, I thought it was the perfect day. I remember saying we couldn't have had a better day."

"Same. I know it was close to school starting again. Maybe the day before?"

Grace nodded thoughtfully. "I think so. Because I'm pretty sure both of us missed the first day of school that year."

"Yeah. We did. I lay in bed and cried all day."

"Yeah. I lay in bed with my phone to my ear talking to you and crying."

Claire smiled faintly as she remembered. They were so close. "Anyway, one of those unexpected storms came up, and we were really scared, because we didn't have a lot of experience on the water. At least I was scared."

"I was scared too. But I remember glancing back and looking at Yolanda, who was behind me, and that look on her face has haunted me for years. I think she was scared."

"Do you think she had a premonition?" Claire asked, feeling goosebumps go down her arms.

"No. But I just remember seeing her looking at the sky, and she didn't look me in the eye after that. It was like she knew that it was going to be worse than what we thought it was going to be. I turned back around and looked at the sky myself, but I just didn't see what she did."

"Interesting. I guess I was in the front, and I didn't see either one of you two. I just, once we decided to row for the shore, rowed as fast as I could. I didn't ever think about the life vest. I wish I would have. That's something else that's haunted me. That stupid life vest."

"Me too. Various times throughout the ride, I could have said, 'Let's put it on.' Or 'How about now.' Or 'We better do this before we head back to the beach.' But I didn't."

"It was one of those rogue waves. The water wasn't especially rough. I personally thought we were going to have plenty of time to get back. But a wave that was bigger than the rest of them just flipped us over."

"Yeah. It happened so fast. Did you see the wave coming?" Grace asked thoughtfully, and the way she asked made Claire think that she had never seen it.

"At the last maybe two or three seconds, I did. But that was way too late. I remember yelling, 'Hang on!' And that was it."

They paused for a moment, and the waitress came with their meals.

Claire, who had been hungry up until that point, wasn't really interested in food. But the scent drifting up was so tantalizing that she picked up her fork without thinking about it.

Grace must've felt the same, because she also pulled her plate toward her and said, "Let's pray."

Claire nodded and then bowed her head while Grace said a short blessing. She didn't say anything profound, and Claire wondered if it was tempting for her to pray for Yolanda, even though she was long gone. For some reason, Claire thought they should. But she knew there was no point in praying for someone who was already dead.

"I remember hearing you yell, 'Hang on,' and then it seemed like almost immediately, the wave picked up our boat, and almost like it had fingers, it tipped us over."

"Yeah. Like it grabbed a hold of the bottom of the boat and dumped us out. You felt that too?" Claire asked, thinking that that was one of the things that she didn't remember very well.

"Yeah. It was clear to me that that was what happened. Except…it was ridiculous. Waves don't have hands. But I never saw Yolanda surface at all. It's like she went down and kept sinking." Grace shook her head, like she didn't understand why Yolanda wouldn't pop back up. "She was a strong swimmer. Stronger than I was."

"Far stronger than me. Swimming was never my thing. As soon as I felt myself coming out of the boat, I thought about my life vest. That was the only thing I was looking for until I grabbed a hold of it. Thankfully, my foot caught it as I was coming out of the boat, and I had the strap in my hand before I even surfaced."

"Mine was right in front of my face when I broke the water. I grabbed it immediately. That, and the kayak, which somehow settled right side up."

"We might not be here to talk about it if it hadn't. You're right. It did. And between us, we had two paddles."

They both sat there thinking. Maybe they were thinking about how they had struggled to get in the boat before either one of them had realized that Yolanda wasn't with them. Then they had called for her while continuing to try to climb in.

"Sometimes I wonder if maybe one of us had dove for her. Or maybe if we had... I don't know. I just knew that I felt like we were pressed for time, and we needed to get to shore. And it was essential that we got back in the boat."

"I felt the same way. And I wonder too—if we would have looked for her, would we have found her?"

"But it wasn't like there was something she could have gotten tangled in. I mean... She had to have sunk down almost immediately."

"Do you think she bumped her head?"

"I've wondered that. Did she get confused? Was she dazed? We just didn't see her? I mean, the wind was blowing pretty hard by then, gusting, with occasional waves. But that big wave was the only wave that was really anything we hadn't dealt with before."

"Yeah. I mean, we did spend what—ten minutes?—looking and calling her name and paddling around. But then we knew we needed to get to shore, and we didn't want to drift."

"Yeah. I remember talking to you about whether or not we were even in the same spot that we were when we capsized. Like we might've been a quarter mile away by then."

"Yeah. We drifted some. But still, she had on a bright pink suit. Surely we would have seen her."

"It was such a bright suit. But..." She sighed. "I suppose the thing that I always worried about the most was that we rode away and she was somehow somewhere where we missed her, and if we would have just seen her, she would have been saved too. But we rode away without her, and she died after we left her."

"That was always my fear as well. I told the police when they talked to us that the boat capsized, and I never saw her come up. Which was the absolute truth. I also told them that we looked around—I mean... I was honest." She shrugged her shoulders. "I always wondered if maybe we missed her."

They were both silent for a bit. There wasn't really any need to talk about anything else. They had gotten to the shore, gotten out of the boat, and immediately called 911.

Someone had been there within twenty minutes, and despite the fact that a random summer storm had come through, they were out on the water looking for her.

Grace picked at her chicken. "We weren't that far from shore. I just... I feel like they should have found her."

They were quiet, because Yolanda's body had never been found.

Finally, Claire asked the question she was most afraid to know the answer to. "Was there anything I could have done to prevent that?"

Grace stared at her. And finally she put her hands up. "I think there are things that we both could have done to prevent it. We could have stayed home that day. We could have insisted on the life vests. But it's not like we talked her out of it. So that should alleviate any guilt. Neither one of us wore one, so it wasn't like we were trying to be safe and trying to hurt her. I guess... We made mistakes. Everyone does. And there were things we could have done that would have prevented the outcome. But I guess I'm just a believer that God allows things to happen for a reason, and for me to sit here and second-guess myself and wish that I would have done differently makes it sound like I know more than God and that I could have done things and handled things better than He did. And to me, that makes me prideful and arrogant."

Claire just stared at Grace with her mouth open. Finally, she said, "I never thought of it that way. That for me to try to change the outcome, even just in my mind, wishing it had been different, made me arrogant, like I thought God couldn't handle it or hadn't handled it well."

"It helps me. Truly. Do I believe that God is in control of everything? Then if I do, He obviously could have changed something about that day. But all I can think is that He wanted Yolanda in heaven with Him." She paused. "But I have spent some time wondering why some people die young and some people don't."

"I guess I just accepted that that's something I'm not going to know until I get to heaven. Why God allows tragedy to befall some people and other people seem to lead charmed lives. It's all confusing and complicated, and I suppose that it will make sense when I get to heaven and maybe have a little bit of the mind of God. But... For now, God says over and over in the Bible how we're just supposed to have faith. That doesn't mean we understand or even that we like what He does—it means we believe that God works everything out for our good and His glory. It means we believe that God is a loving God even when it seems like He's not. It means that we believe that God is in charge of our lives and protects us from our own stupidity sometimes, and then other times... He doesn't. And I don't know why. I can't explain it. I just know faith is a huge part of that. And without faith, we can't please God."

"Wow. That was deep. It's all about faith. Why can't I see that? I want to have everything explained to me." Grace smiled gently, and then she said, "Something you said about your grandma struck me. It was that she was with Jesus, and you were going to be happy for that. I never thought about that with Yolanda. I know she was a Christian. And I'm sure she's in heaven. But it never occurred to me that she was probably happier than I ever was—in heaven with Jesus. The last dozen years or so, I've struggled and cried and been hurt and dealt with divorce and saw my life fall apart and have been through trial and tragedy, and... Yolanda's been happy in heaven all this time. Why would I wish any different for her?"

"That's such a great point. Wishing that she was still with us is kind of saying that we think that somehow she would be happier with us than with Jesus? That's crazy."

"And I got that idea from you. So thanks."

"I wish I could take credit for it, but it was Grandma. When she was given her six-months-to-live sentence, she was happy. She was excited, even. She was going to see Jesus. The only thing that made her sad was the fact that I was sad about it. And I tried not to be, because I knew I was the thing that was bringing her down. Otherwise, she would have gone skipping out of that doctor's office and probably jumping up and tapping her heels together. That's the kind of attitude that she had."

"That's amazing. I hope I have that kind of attitude when I get news like that."

"Somehow I think it's a lot harder for the people who are left behind. We have to live life without the people that make everything familiar. We kind of have our anchor set on the familiar, and we depend on the people around us. And on the one hand, God gives us people to live this life with, and for that exact reason, so we have someone to depend on. But... I think sometimes they take the place of God. At least, that's what I figured out for me in my life. That my world gets tilted and almost upside down because I put my trust in the wrong thing—in people instead of God."

Grace nodded. "That's good." She smiled a bit. "For a while, I didn't think I was going to be able to eat my chicken, but I feel my appetite has come back."

"Same. I think it might be the smell. It is divine. But we went on a carriage ride with Becky and Rodney and then flew kites along the lake, and I didn't eat nearly enough food."

"Wait until they're both teenagers—you're going to need to buy a grocery store in order to keep from getting eaten out of house and home."

"Oh goodness. Maybe I'll be happy at some point that my husband has them over the summer, so I can get an extra job just to pay for the food I'm going to need in my house."

"I don't know how people with big families do it."

"They need a garden. So they can feed their kids. And with all those kids, they have plenty of free labor to grow and weed and work in the garden."

They laughed together.

They chatted about the weather and about a few things in town, and how Raspberry Ridge really needed a restaurant or something.

"It's too bad Lauren's mom isn't feeling well. Since the bakery closed down a few years ago, it just hasn't been the same."

"I agree. No one could bake like Lauren's mom."

"Except Lauren. Lauren actually made a few things that I liked better."

"I guess I'll always be partial to my grandma's homemade bread. Unfortunately, she passed before I truly learned her secrets. My bread doesn't turn out like hers."

"I think that's what makes the people in our lives special. If we could just do everything that they did, we wouldn't miss them."

"I suppose you're right. Still, Lauren's mom made cheese bread that was just absolutely divine."

They chatted a bit more, and then Claire apologized. "I wish I could stay longer. But Josiah is making barbecue ribs for us tonight, and I don't know how I'm going to eat another bite, but I definitely don't want to miss it. He's expecting me to be there."

"Of course. I... I think you and Josiah might have something going on."

Claire knew her cheeks had to be beet red. "I hope so. I can't imagine anyone being more supportive of someone than what Josiah was of me during this whole situation. I'm not talking just since Grandma died, but when she was diagnosed with cancer. It's true that he knew and didn't tell me, but that was because Grandma didn't want me to know. And he respected that. But no one could have been more supportive or kind or better in any way than what Josiah was."

"I guess you know by now that kind of man isn't easy to find."

"No. It's not. And if he happens to be funny, and handy, and..." Claire blushed even more red. "A good kisser."

Grace laughed. "You've known that since you were what—fourteen?"

"Something like that. And yeah, it was a little bit of knowledge I had tucked away."

"He's probably gotten better over the years."

Claire paused, and then she let the words come out. "I hope I get to find out."

Twenty-Two

"Oh my goodness, I had the best day," Claire said, and Josiah wanted to reach across between the chairs and pull her from hers onto his lap.

But Dan and Lana were sitting across the fire from them in their own chairs, and her children might wonder what was going on with the adults if he did what he wanted to.

So he didn't, but he contented himself with looking at her and enjoying the happiness that practically radiated from her face.

They had taken the boat out on the lake. They'd flown kites again, hiked along the beach, walked up as far as they possibly could, had a picnic, and walked back. They'd even taken another carriage ride. Plus, they'd made twenty loaves of bread and delivered one to every house in Raspberry Ridge.

The kids had helped work in the flower beds some, and he'd gotten a little bit of work done in the kitchen, although he still wasn't done with it.

But how could he resist when Claire invited him to go along with her and her children? He wasn't going to say no. If she didn't want him, she shouldn't ask.

They'd finally gotten around to the campfire—one last one before the funeral. Tomorrow everything would be about Grandma, celebrating her life, attending her funeral, and burying her. It was sure to be a hard day, and he was making his barbecue ribs for that evening, so they'd have something to look forward to. Maybe they'd have another bonfire.

But then, on Sunday, Claire was taking her kids to Pennsylvania to meet her ex. Her ex had talked her into doing it over the weekend so he didn't have to take off work. She'd figured it was the least she could do since he had agreed to allow her the extra week.

Claire had said that Josiah didn't need to go with her. He would have the entire house to himself to work on the kitchen to his heart's content. He was ready to get it done, but in the meantime, he was hoping he could have it—if not done, at least not looking like the chaos that it did now.

Regardless, it had been a good week, not just a good day.

"Do we have to go to Dad's?" Lana said, and her question did not surprise Josiah at all. Instead, he'd been expecting this all week. Claire had gone out of her way to make sure that the kids had a week of fun with her, and she'd been so successful, so happy, so joyful, that he couldn't imagine anyone wanting to leave her. Of course, he was biased too.

"I don't want to go either. I want to stay here with you. I hate Boston." Dan held a stick with a marshmallow on the end of it, and it was far enough back from the fire that Josiah could tell him that it was never going to get brown and melted, but he figured that Dan could learn that. It wouldn't hurt anything for him to figure it out on his own.

"Well, I would love for both of you to stay here all summer, but your dad wants to see you two. He misses you. He's been looking forward to having you come."

Josiah admired Claire. He knew that she didn't necessarily want to say those things about their dad. After all, their dad hadn't loved them enough to not cheat, to not break the family apart, to not screw up when he'd been given a second chance. Still, she wasn't trashing their dad. She was...trying to help them love him. But some things just couldn't be helped.

"He can come here if he wants to see us," Lana said, crossing her legs and looking much more mature than her thirteen years.

"Well, maybe you could invite him here. But... He's got his own life back in Boston. He has his work, and..." Here, Claire hesitated. And then she said, "He might have something to tell you about the family that he's trying to build."

She had told Josiah that one of her friends from Boston had told her that her ex was getting very serious with a woman who already had two children. They were younger, and Claire had told Josiah that she was very grateful that they were younger—they weren't as old as her children. She worried some about blended families and stepsiblings molesting the younger ones. It wasn't something that she'd heard about from anyone that he knew, but he could understand her fear. Especially since she was a thousand miles away in Michigan and wouldn't be around if her children needed her immediately.

She had confided in Josiah that she had a couple of girlfriends she knew she could call, but it wasn't the same as her being there.

He had gently asked if maybe she felt like she needed to move back to Boston.

She'd shaken her head immediately, saying that she wanted to be here, in her grandma's old house, living in the town she'd grown up in. She wanted her kids to be able to spend the school years here, at least.

"If you loved us, you wouldn't make us go," Dan said belligerently.

"It's because I love you that I am making you go. And actually, it's your dad that's making you go. If your dad says you can stay here, go ahead. I'll keep you. I would prefer that, actually."

There. That's where she drew the line. She wasn't going to take the fall for her ex splitting the family up completely.

"Fine. Let me have your phone, I'll call Dad now." Lana held her hand out, and Claire shrugged and held out the phone, but she made her daughter come get it.

Her daughter disappeared, and Dan jumped up, running after her.

"I don't know what to do. Please tell me I'm not screwing them up forever."

"I think Ted already did that." He didn't mean to be all gloom and doom, but a divorce would leave scars, no matter what. He couldn't lie and tell her that it wouldn't. She knew it. She was looking to him to not lie.

"I just wish there was something I could do to undo all the painful, hard things that he's done."

He nodded and didn't bother to remind her that the kids would grow through the pain and suffering. It would be hard, no questions about that, but they would grow. They would learn. There would be things that would be different in their lives because of the trials they went through. Claire knew it, though, and he didn't have to rub it in.

Lana came stomping back just a few minutes later.

"Dad wants to talk to you," she said, handing the phone to Claire.

Claire exchanged a look with Josiah before she took the phone from Lana.

She held it up to the ear closest to Josiah, and he could hear her ex's voice clearly.

"What are you trying to do—turn the children against me? I let you have an extra week, and all of a sudden, they don't want to come here at all? What's wrong with you? I trusted you."

He wanted to roll his eyes. A cheater giving his ex-spouse a hard time because he couldn't trust her? That was rich. And he also wanted to jump to Claire's defense. She'd wanted to create memories for herself, not to make things harder for her husband.

"I didn't do anything I wouldn't have done with them if they had spent the entire summer with me. We just had to cram it all into a few days, because my grandma's funeral is tomorrow. We'll be spending the day burying her. And then Sunday, we're driving to Pennsylvania to meet you."

He was gratified to hear the calmness and peace in Claire's voice. He made a mental note to tell her that she'd handled it well.

Somehow, some of the anger in Ted's voice had defused. "I don't like my kids calling me and asking if they can stay and telling me they don't want to come to Boston."

"I don't like my kids coming to me and crying and asking me when Dad is going to come home and why he doesn't live with us anymore."

"Really? You have to go there?"

"I'm sorry. My point is, both of us have to deal with things we don't want to."

"You don't have to hold it against me for the rest of my life. Just because you weren't a good enough wife, and I needed my sexual urges satisfied, and you weren't enough—is that my fault?"

He heard Claire suck in her breath. He could see the hurt pierce right through her eyes. He wanted to grab the phone and smash it to smithereens, but he just sat in his chair.

"The children have a right to their opinion and to express what they want. I told them if you changed your mind and didn't want them for the summer, I would keep them. Otherwise, I told them, in no uncertain terms, that we would be going to Pennsylvania to meet you on Sunday. Is there anything else you wanted?"

Her voice was completely devoid of all warmth. There was no friendliness or engagement in it. She was just talking because she had to.

Maybe because she wanted to hide from him, or maybe because she wanted to keep him from being able to hurt her again.

"No. But I don't want the children calling me and asking if they can stay there for the summer. That was rude and underhanded. And I don't appreciate it. Goodbye."

Claire kept the phone to her ear for just a bit longer, and Josiah waited.

Finally she lowered it, not even bothering to look to see if it was off. It was clear that her ex-husband had hung up on her.

"He said no, didn't he?" Lana said, her arms crossed over her chest, her foot sticking out, and her whole body showing her displeasure.

"He loves you. He wants to see you."

Josiah was impressed. After the insult that her husband had unfairly lodged against her, he couldn't believe that she wasn't curled up crying somewhere or railing against him. But instead, she was saying the same thing she had said before—that he loved them, which probably was true.

"I'm going to run away. I'm not going to go back to Boston," Dan said, and he started to stomp away.

"Hey there. Hold on a second," Josiah said. Maybe the fact that he had interjected himself into the conversation made Dan stop, or maybe Dan just wanted someone to stop him.

Anyway, his tone didn't hold any heat or anger. And he was surprised when Dan actually listened.

"I guess you can look at this two different ways. You can look at it like you're angry about what you have to do, and you can ruin tonight because of what you think you're going to have to do a couple of days from now, because you can't get your way for the summer. Or you can decide that you're going to be happy in the moment, which is right now, and you're not going to let the things that you're not happy about ruin tonight. And tomorrow, and the ride to Pennsylvania with your mom. I guess you're a little young to be thinking about stuff like that, but it's your life. You can enjoy it, or not."

"But I'm mad," Dan said, sounding like he hadn't heard a word Josiah had said.

"I guess I'm a little bit mad right now too, although maybe for different reasons."

He didn't look at Claire, but he could feel her eyes on him. "But this is a beautiful night, I love bonfires, and I've had such a great week with you guys, I'd like to enjoy a little bit more time before you have to leave. And I don't like that, but I'm not going to allow it to ruin tonight."

"You didn't get your marshmallow done," Lana said, and it was actually said in a kind of nice tone. Maybe she'd figured out that the only familiar thing she was going to have in Boston was her brother, and maybe she should develop a relationship with him. Or, more likely, she'd heard what Josiah had said, and it made sense to her.

The kids came back over, Dan picked his stick back up, and they sat down. But the mood was ruined.

Claire leaned over and said softly, "Thanks."

He probably shouldn't have said it. He had no right—they didn't have any kind of agreement between the two of them, and he had no hold on her—but he leaned over toward her and said, "I heard what your husband said, and I wanted to grab a hold of his throat and slam him into the ground. You are way more than enough."

She stared at him, then shook her head, and didn't say anything.

He didn't mind. But this was the day before her grandma's funeral, and while he had other things he wanted to say to her, he took his own advice that he'd given the children and didn't spoil the evening by pushing a romance that she might not want on her.

She finally took the kids in for the night, and he put the fire out and headed home.

It wasn't super late, and he wasn't surprised to see his dad still up when he got there.

He greeted his dad and asked how his day was and asked about his mom too.

His dad chatted for a bit, and then he threw a bombshell at Josiah.

"I've decided to retire."

"I wasn't expecting that," Josiah said immediately, pausing in getting the dishes out of the dishwasher and putting them away, and he stopped, leaning against the counter. "Is there any particular reason why?" he asked, wondering if there was something that his parents were going to tell him about his mom's health.

"I'm sure you've noticed that your mom isn't getting better. Each day, she seems to get a little worse. The hospital offered me a package, and I took it. We're going to move to New Mexico, and we'll be selling the house."

"Wow. That's a lot to digest."

"We assumed you would be coming with us. They need handymen in New Mexico just as much as they do here. I mean, they probably don't have as many yachts," his dad said, his eyes sparkling with that little hint of laughter that always lurked around the corner with his dad.

"I'm sure they probably don't. But you're right. They have buildings of some kind."

"Yeah. And you're industrious, you do good work, and I don't think you'd have trouble finding a job."

"I don't think I would either. But maybe you and Mom want to have some time with the two of you."

"We wouldn't turn it down, but we didn't want you to think we were tossing you out on the curb. I suppose I should have waited for your mom, because she could say it all better. But we've been talking about it for a while, and I just turned in my papers at work to say that

I'm retiring and taking the package they offered. I guess it was on my mind, so I wanted to tell you."

"Thanks. I hope that I'm not too much of a nuisance."

He knew he wasn't. He had helped with his mom. If he hadn't been there, they probably would have had to hire a nurse for her on the days his dad had to stay in Blueberry Beach. So there was no question in his mind about whether or not his parents wanted him. But to New Mexico... He wasn't interested. And it wasn't just because he loved Raspberry Ridge and the town he'd grown up in. It was...partly because of Claire. And his hope that maybe there was something growing between them. Something more than just being friends.

Still, even if it weren't for Claire, he didn't want to move. He was happy where he was, although...it was sad to think about his parents leaving.

Was this how Claire had felt with her grandma? Like her world had been rocked a little bit, and everything that she'd thought was going to be happening was changing?

"You know you've been more help than anything. I guess your mom and I just assumed you'd be coming. It...is going to be a surprise to her that you think you might not."

"I'm pretty sure I'm not. I love it here. I love you guys, and I'll miss you. For sure. But I can't imagine living anywhere but Raspberry Ridge."

That wasn't entirely true. He couldn't imagine living somewhere else, unless Claire was beside him. Boston, perhaps, although he wouldn't want to. Boston just seemed dark to him, although he'd never even been there. Maybe he'd like it better than what he thought he would.

"Would you be interested in buying the house?" his dad asked. "Your mom and I haven't talked to a real estate agent yet, but we were going to do that on Monday. We figured we'd list it. With the market the way it is, we didn't think it would last long. Plus, we're going to price it slightly below market value for a quick sale. I'll be done at the hospital in two weeks, and we're already looking at real estate in New Mexico."

"Wow. You guys aren't messing around."

"She didn't tell you, but at her last appointment, the doctor recommended she go somewhere warmer. He said that another winter like we had this winter would do more harm than good. It made sense to us. But it just took a while before all the pieces fit together. The hospital just happened to offer this retirement package to those of us who have enough years to qualify for it. After that, it was pretty much a no-brainer."

"Yeah. I can see how that's perfect for you guys. And maybe it'll be nice to have a few years of empty nesting, without your kid underfoot all the time."

"You've never been underfoot. We've always appreciated you, and if you wanted to come, we'd find a place where we could all live together. If you are truly not interested in going with us, we might find an over-55 community where we'd involve ourselves and enjoy a few years of activities."

"The more active you stay, the healthier you'll be."

"I wonder if your mom might not be healthier if we got her doing some exercise. I thought once we moved to New Mexico, I'd see if we couldn't try a few things."

"I think that's a good idea," Josiah said. He supposed he was a little bit in shock. It was a lot to take in.

"You didn't answer me about the house."

"No. I'm sorry. I... Could I have a day or so to think about it?"

"Sure. I told you we're going to list on Monday, but we can tell the real estate agent that we have one person who might make an offer on it before it goes live."

"That'd be fine. How much are you asking for it?"

His dad told him the number, and he nodded.

"I'll think about it, and I'll try to let you know by Monday." That didn't give him a whole lot of time, but he'd be working in Claire's kitchen for a good bit of that time, and he'd have a lot of time to think.

His first thought was that Claire's old farmhouse was big enough for him and her and her kids together, but... He couldn't move in with Claire. That wouldn't look right. Not unless they were married, and he hadn't even declared his feelings for her yet, let alone talked about a long-term relationship. Marriage wasn't even on the horizon.

His dad said good night and then went to bed, leaving Josiah with his thoughts.

He could buy his parents' house and probably would. But if he and Claire were going to get together, it was obvious that they would live at her grandma's farmhouse. He couldn't imagine her wanting to move to town when being out in the country was so much nicer, not just for her, with the garden and the chickens and the beautiful views of the green hills, but also for the kids. The bonfire, the easy walking distance to the lake, their own private beach.

No, Claire would definitely want to stay at her grandma's house. But she might surprise him.

He was thinking like he'd already told her how he felt and that he was already thinking about where they would spend the rest of their lives together. He needed to stop getting the cart ahead of the horse. And he wasn't going to get anything hitched up tomorrow, since it was her grandma's funeral. And then she was leaving on Sunday to take her kids, which would be another hard day for her. And it would take her a little while to recover from that next week.

He was looking at several weeks before he even spoke to her about it.

He might as well just tell his dad he would buy the house, and then he would be responsible for selling it or renting it out or something. He wasn't sure. On that thought, he finished up in the kitchen and decided to call it a night.

Twenty-Three

"You didn't have to wait for me," Claire said as she wearily got out of her car to see Josiah standing on the porch steps.

The roof was still held up by two-by-fours, but he leaned against the post with his arms over his chest.

He started coming down the steps as she got out. "I wasn't really waiting on you. I spent the last couple of days working as hard as I could on the kitchen, and I kind of wanted to see what you thought about it."

"Is it finished?" she asked, slamming the door shut and feeling tired to her very bones. Her kids were in Boston, and her husband had surprised both of them with new phones, without checking with her, of course. They had originally decided that their kids would be sixteen before they would be allowed to have iPhones, and Dan was only ten.

But she supposed this was the way parenting went when a couple split up. Everything they'd agreed on went out the window too. She wasn't sure. She didn't like the fact that her kids had phones, but she did like the fact that Lana had messaged her and let her know that they had arrived safely.

She had both of their numbers and had asked them to check in with her every day.

Whether they would or not, she wasn't sure, but she was going to try to enforce that. She would have set that up before they left if she would have realized what her husband was going to do.

"It's not done, but I'd like you to look at it," Josiah said, coming down and stopping in front of her. "Did you have a good trip?"

"Yeah. I have a surprising amount of peace about this. I hated to see my children leave, but yeah, I have peace." She'd had that same peace through her grandmother's funeral, the graveside service, and the mingling at the viewing as well. She was almost looking forward to the summer. And Josiah was the reason.

"Well, then let's go see the kitchen."

"Could you wait a moment, please?" she asked, putting a hand on his forearm.

He stopped immediately.

"I have a confession to make."

"Okay?" he said, sounding curious and confused at the same time. He turned but did not move closer to her. She supposed that he was respecting her space. Or maybe respecting the fact that she'd had a lot of things happen to her in the last week—the last year—and maybe he was thinking that she needed to have time to recover. Taking her children to Pennsylvania had been hard, and maybe she shouldn't make any rash decisions after such painful things had happened, but she'd been leaning toward this before anything had happened to her grandma and before her kids left.

"I lied to you," she said, looking up at him, thankful for the porch light which shone on their faces, allowing her to see his expression.

It had been brutal driving to Pennsylvania yesterday and back today. It had been even more brutal saying goodbye to her children. They'd eaten breakfast together, a late one, since Ted was not an early riser, which was just fine with her, because the hotel pool had been open, and she and the kids had taken an early morning swim while he slept. She'd cherished every second. Anyway, after their late breakfast, she had watched them go, kissing them and telling them she loved them without crying, but it had been a little while before she'd been able to get in her car and see where she was going through the tears.

"You lied to me?" he asked, narrowing his eyes, maybe not looking annoyed exactly but definitely confused.

"Yeah. You remember that truth or dare game? And our kiss?" She didn't know whether she should say this or not. But she'd decided on the way home that her new beginning was going to include her being brave about certain things. This was one of those things.

"I guess we've established the fact that I had some pretty fond memories around that. I understand that you don't."

"That's just it. I lied to you. I really, really liked that kiss. I talked about it for months afterward. I really wanted another one. I wanted more. But... I guess you just weren't part of the clique that I was in in high school, and I decided that... I don't know. But it was the best kiss I'd ever had."

"Maybe that's because it was your first one," he said, and she could almost see the thoughts whirling through his head as he softened toward her, and his free hand came up and landed on her shoulder. She thought maybe he knew where she was going with this.

"I don't know. I do know that you were the first boy I'd ever kissed, and... I was hoping that you would also be the last."

It wasn't exactly a marriage proposal, but it was letting him know how she felt. Kind of. In an almost-brave kind of way.

He swallowed, almost like his throat was dry and he needed to force his throat to work.

"Yeah. I like that idea." He smiled a little and then said, "Almost as much as I like the idea that you were my first kiss, and I'd like for you to be my last."

She smiled. That was what she was hoping he would say.

"I...know you don't need any practice. You were really good the first time. But I thought maybe I needed some. Do you mind?" she asked, taking a brave step forward and putting her hand around his neck, pressing against him and tugging down at the same time.

"I don't mind at all. In fact, I feel like you're wrong. I do need a little practice. Maybe a lot of practice. Maybe a lifetime's worth of practice."

"Yeah. That's what I thought too."

She wasn't sure whether he lowered his head, or she forced him to, or maybe she just stretched really high on her tiptoes, but somehow they were kissing, and it was perfect, just like the last time. The first time.

Twenty-Four

Two weeks later

"You did an amazing job on the kitchen. I love it. And I have a feeling that Grandma would have loved it too."

"I have a feeling that Grandma knew that she wasn't going to be around to enjoy it, and she wanted to make sure that you were taken care of."

Claire smiled, put her arm around Josiah, and kissed his cheek. She wanted to ask him to marry her, and she wanted to do it soon. He had already told her that his parents were moving to New Mexico, and he was going to buy their house. She wanted to tell him that there was no need for him to do that. That they could just move into the farmhouse together. But they would need to get married, of course. She wasn't quite sure that he loved her that much yet.

Or maybe that he wanted to take that big of a chance on her. Regardless, she'd enjoyed the last two weeks together with him. And there was a part of her that was kind of happy that her kids were in Boston.

The summer stretched out, exciting and anticipatory, with Josiah by her side. She'd thanked him over and over for the steadfast presence that he'd been during Grandma's illness and death and her children leaving, and he'd just shaken his head like he didn't understand what the big deal was.

They'd gone through her grandma's will, with no surprises. The house, along with a set amount of money to finish fixing it up, had been left to her. Everything else that her grandma owned had been divided up with the rest of the family.

Grandma had made one stipulation. She wanted the farm to be called Verdant Hills Farm.

That hadn't been a problem, and the next day, Josiah had made her a sign for the end of her driveway with "Verdant Hills Farm" written on it.

It hung there now.

"I think the kids will have a lot of fun baking bread in this kitchen this winter." She turned to Josiah. "And I hope you will be here to enjoy eating it."

"I don't know why you think I'm going somewhere," he said, dropping a kiss on her forehead and letting his lips linger there.

She closed her eyes, just enjoying the feel of him close, knowing that he had zero plans of leaving her. And Josiah was not the kind of man who left easily.

His parents were packed up and getting ready to move to New Mexico that week. He had told her that he might need to go with them to get them settled, but so far, they hadn't asked him to.

Her thoughts were interrupted by her phone ringing. She felt a new urgency every time it rang, now that her children were a thousand miles away, and she hadn't quite gotten over the idea that they might need her.

"It's Ted," she said, looking at Josiah. She bit her lip. Ted didn't typically call her, especially not on a Tuesday afternoon. This was definitely out of the ordinary.

"Hello?" she said, putting the phone on speaker so Josiah could hear too. He had great hearing, and even if she had been holding it to her ear, he probably would have been able to hear anyway. He had surprised her greatly at the campfire two weeks ago when he'd heard the insult that her ex had lobbed at her and had said what he had.

She hadn't wanted him to hear. Because she felt like it wasn't true. It didn't matter what she did—her ex wasn't satisfied with her. It was like he needed variety or something, but everything was always her fault. Josiah had seen through that immediately.

"Claire. The kids are driving me crazy. I stayed home from work today, because yesterday they made a huge mess in the condo, and the landlord and my neighbors are complaining. It's like you've been letting them run wild or something."

"No. It's been very civilized here. We even have indoor plumbing."

"Very funny. Anyway, Justine, my girlfriend, is stressed out about it. Her kids are being badly influenced by yours, and I think two weeks was more than enough time with us. I'll see them again at Christmas."

"Wait, what?"

"Didn't you hear me? I want to meet you again. They're coming back. You can bring them back for Christmas, and I'll see them then."

"Okay. We'll meet tomorrow?" she said, surprised and not wanting to let this opportunity slip away. She certainly wasn't going to turn this down.

"Yeah, unless you want to meet late tonight."

"Sure. Late tonight is fine," she said as Josiah nodded his head. He might not be able to go with her. Someone would need to stay and make sure the chickens had food and water, unless they fed them extra and made sure they put extra water in before they left.

"All right. Same hotel, tonight, as soon as you can get there."

"All right. I'll see you tonight." She managed to keep the excitement out of her voice until she swiped off the phone.

Then she squealed and jumped, throwing her arms around Josiah's neck.

He caught her and didn't complain at all when her lips found his.

She almost got distracted by the kiss, but then she squealed again and said, "Can we put extra water out for the chickens? Then you can come too."

"But we'll have to stay overnight."

"We'll get two hotel rooms." Then she paused and thought, *This is really not the time.* But she didn't let that stop her. "Would you marry me? Please?"

That probably wasn't the way that was supposed to go, but he laughed. And then he said, "Sure. Today?"

"Well, I just made plans for today, but maybe tomorrow evening?"

He smiled, and then he said, "Maybe we could hold off until Thursday."

"All right. Thursday. I'm going to hold you to that," she said, poking a finger into his chest.

"All right. You make sure you do. In the meantime, if I'm going to marry you, I think you ought to finish painting the outside of the house."

"Maybe I can get my husband to help me," she said, and then, feeling a little saucy, she kissed his chin before she reached up on her tiptoes and spent a longer time kissing his lips.

He kissed her back, and neither one of them were laughing when they finally broke apart.

"If we're going to make it to Pennsylvania tonight, you need to stop doing that."

"All right. Just because I want to see my kids. But in a few days, I'm going to expect you to do that all night long."

"All right. I think that's something we can work out."

She smiled, and then Josiah took her hand, and they walked outside together to do the chickens before they left to get her kids. All of a sudden, the verdant hills and sparkling sky held a whole new, exciting promise for her. The promise of the summer with her children, and... who knew? Maybe there would be more kids.

The thought made her smile even bigger.

Join Jessie's list and be the first to know about new releases and sales on her books!

Get your copy of Between the Shady Groves, the next book in the Raspberry Ridge series, in which a grieving and abandoned Lauren revives her mother's legacy as a new romance blossoms. Both are threatened by the unexpected return of her ex-husband. Can Lauren hold onto the fragile happiness she's built?

Lauren Knodel pushed the key into the old-fashioned lock and wiggled it gently. There was a knack to this old thing, and she finally felt it click. Then, she turned it, and the lock sprung.

She braced herself, taking a deep breath and closing her eyes for a moment, before she pushed open the door to her mother's bakery—empty and abandoned on the main street of Raspberry Ridge—and stepped inside.

It had been years since she'd been in here, but everything looked the same. Her mother always left those big bowls on the back shelf. Her mixer was spotlessly clean. It was her pride and joy. An expensive piece of equipment that she had saved for years to buy when Lauren had been younger. Lauren remembered the celebration when her mom had finally been able to purchase it and how she had guarded it fiercely, protecting it and yet showing it off by making everything visible from the other side of the counter.

In fact, almost everything that her mom did in the bakery was visible from the other side of the counter. It was one of the reasons why folks in Raspberry Ridge had always loved her shop. It wasn't just a bakeshop with amazing smells and tantalizing desserts. It was a place where one could go to learn, be entertained, see what was on the menu, and actually see it be prepared. There were no secrets.

Even now, a yeasty smell rose around her, mixed in with the dust. A little bit of vanilla, cinnamon, and Lauren could close her eyes and see her mother pulling a tray of puffy golden cinnamon buns out of one of the double ovens built into the wall.

She would have the icing ready and smooth it on while the buns were still hot. There would be a line of people waiting to purchase them, and the cinnamon buns would be gone before the pan cooled.

Her mother had a touch, a gift, and her mom had always said that Lauren had inherited it. Lauren hadn't wanted to have anything to do with it.

She sighed, closing her eyes and stepping in, closing the door behind her before opening her eyes again and looking around trying to figure out what had changed.

Her. She had changed. She had grown from the spoiled, immature, egotistical girl who thought she knew everything but really knew nothing.

Deep inside, she had been scared and intimidated and petrified, and the tragedy that she had been a part of had attached to her, chasing her from this small lakeside community to the city of Cincinnati, where she worked for a while before she fell in love and got married.

And then, after three miscarriages, a lot of miscommunication, and the death of her mom—she decided to pack up and come back.

She spent years caring for her mother. All for naught.

Now, she needed to figure out what to do with this, her mother's pride and joy. The shop where her mom had lovingly prepared each and every delectable dessert and baked good that she'd happily sold to her friends and neighbors. She fed her daughter here, made a living here, and they lived in the back and upstairs. There was a bit of a backyard with a shady grove of peach trees providing shade in the summer, delicious fruit in the fall, and the promise of both of those things all winter long, as the bare branches reached to the sky.

Even now, the tiny fruits were growing, ripening, getting ready to burst into flavor and juicy deliciousness in another month or two.

The trees had been neglected for years, and Lauren had no idea whether they would bear good fruit in their neglected state or not.

Her mom had always cultivated them, pruned them, and sometimes even sprayed them. But Lauren had done nothing. She had been too busy caring for her mom and ignoring her failing marriage while it fell apart.

Her jaw tightened, and she stopped thinking about peach trees so that she could stop thinking about her marriage. It was as dead as the branches in winter.

Even if she didn't have an official divorce yet. Cannon, her husband, would soon file. He wasn't the kind of man who would be alone for long. Successful and charismatic, good at his job, building a million-dollar business from nothing, he would be a catch for someone. Lauren turned away, her eyes sweeping the storefront once again.

She didn't know what to do. She couldn't go back. And she didn't know how to move forward. Unless she opened her mother's shop again. But...could she?

She didn't know how to run a business, had never paid attention. Her husband had done it, her mama had done it before that. But her? She worked at a job, but she knew that running a business was different. There was so much more responsibility. A person didn't just work the job, they had to do pricing and inventory and taxes and all the backend things, like making sure that there was insurance, and what about employees?

She had no idea how to do any of it.

Not for the first time, she wished for Cannon's wise advice. He was a good man. A really good man. But...the years of taking care of her mom and the miscarriages that she'd endured before that had taken their toll on their marriage, and their communication had become almost nonexistent. They allowed their relationship to die. And she walked away.

Is that what happened? she questioned herself, because she wasn't sure anymore. Losing her mom had taken the last of her strength, the last of her will to explore and challenge and thrive. She just wanted to curl into a ball and do nothing. What was this? Depression? This weight on her chest, this dark cloud hanging over her, and the idea that life would never be fun again.

Maybe it was the idea that she had missed so much of her mom's life because she'd been selfish. She pursued what she wanted and hadn't considered how devastated her mom must have felt to have her only daughter leave, and not just leave, but leave with a big smile on her face and an attitude of "this town isn't good enough for me, I need to find something big enough to hold me."

She had basically thumbed her nose at everything her mama built, the town that she moved to to raise her, and the friends and neighbors who had supported her throughout her childhood.

She walked over to the place where the counter folded up. She lifted up the moveable piece, like she had a million times in childhood, and slipped through so she stood behind the counter, where her mom practically lived.

She took a few more steps to her mother's prized mixer, the huge one that sat on the low shelf built just for it and could hold enough dough to feed the town.

It was the one that her mom had used every morning after that glorious day when she had finally been able to afford to buy it.

Lauren tested it with her fingers, sliding them over it, seeing the dust rub off the mixer, and thinking about her mom and the many hours that this mixer had spent turned on in the kitchen, with townspeople laughing and joking at the few tables that were set around, or sitting at the bar, while her mom made them their specialty coffees, getting more and more complicated over the years, and shared laughter and tears and life together.

Her mom had known just how to do all of that. To handle it all so perfectly. To balance the intricacies of making a business profitable, making a living from it, and still having friendships and feelings and making people feel like her shop was their second home.

But now, her mom was gone. All the wisdom, all the recipes, all the knowledge. It was all just memories. Whatever was left.

She took a breath, and her stomach growled. She realized she hadn't eaten since the day before, sometime. Maybe breakfast? She wasn't sure.

She had driven here from Cincinnati and slept upstairs. The apartment held memories too, but not like this did. This was where life happened.

She had bought a few groceries at the store in Blueberry Beach, the last one she passed before she got here. Enough groceries to make her mom's specialty. Nutella banana bread. It was easy but so, so good. It had been her favorite back in high school. She didn't know when Nutella came out, but her mom had discovered it at some point, and it instantly skyrocketed to Lauren's favorite baked good of all time. She had gotten the recipe from her mom, and it had become her signature bread. That, along with the cheesy bread that her mom made so well—she had a knack for it too, and most people said she made it even better than her mom.

That would take a little while, but on a whim, she had brought the ingredients for that as well.

First, she needed to clean the dust off the equipment and the counters and…wade through the memories so that she could possibly pick up the pieces of her life.

She thought about her husband, the life she had expected to build with him. It was her fault as much as his. She had to take the blame where it was due. She had been devastated by the miscarriages, and…it seemed like he didn't care. And then, with her mom getting sick, she moved her mom in and put all of her being into caring for her mom. There hadn't been anything left for her husband. That had been on her.

But her husband had been busy working, making his business successful, and basically paying for everything. She had quit her job as a teacher so that she could stay home and be with her mom. She hadn't even talked to her husband about it; she had just done it.

He'd not complained. He was a good man. Still, it was hard to forgive him for the fact that he couldn't comfort her in her loss. Not over their children, not over her mom. He just kept working.

It irritated her to the point she couldn't stand it anymore.

Plus, she had a deep longing to come home. And now, she was finally here. All she had to do was figure out how she was going to make a living. If she could open the baked goods shop and make it as successful as her mom had over the years. Or was the era of the small mom-and-pop bakery completely over?

Sign up for Jessie's newsletter! Get a free book, access to exclusive bonus content, get fun and funny updates on her life on the farm and more!

A Gift from Jessie

View this code through your smart phone camera to be taken to a page where you can download a FREE ebook when you sign up to get updates from Jessie Gussman! Find out why people say, "Jessie's is the only newsletter I open and read" and "You make my day brighter. Love, love, love reading your newsletters. I don't know where you find time to write books. You are so busy living life. A true blessing." and "I know from now on that I can't be drinking my morning coffee while reading your newsletter – I laughed so hard I sprayed it out all over the table!"

Claim your free book from Jessie!